# The Highwaymen

The Chicolote highwayman, notable for his odd habit of returning his ill-gotten gains after terrorizing passengers and stagecoach drivers, had long been responsible for disrupting coach travel and gold shipments along the line.

Now he was dead, or so the story went, but his body was never found and the stick-ups continued as before. Could there be a second man imitating him? Or perhaps more?

The robberies always happened on the same stretch of the same dangerous road, with the same precision. The banks were getting nervous about sending anything of value on the Chicolote and the passengers feared for their safety. Someone had to stop the hold-ups. . . .

It was a job for Laredo.

# The Highwaymen

Owen G. Irons

A Black Horse Western

ROBERT HALE · LONDON

ISBN 978-0-7090-8978-0

Robert Hale Limited
Clerkenwell House
Clerkenwell Green
London EC1R 0HT

www.halebooks.com

*

Typeset by
Derek Doyle & Associates, Shaw Heath
Printed and bound in Great Britain by
CPI Antony Rowe, Chippenham and Eastbourne

# ONE

Dane Hoffman had been driving on the Chicolote Stageline for nearly six years, but he had never seen this one before. As he crested the Fairmont cut-off, the full moonlight showed what seemed to be a dead man lying in the road and he reined his team in sharply. From inside the darkened coach a man's voice – Mr Torrance's – shouted out.

'What now!' He was an irritable little man with a florid face and a plain, well-padded wife who looked down her nose at the employees of the Chicolote Stageline as she probably did with any other inferiors she was unfortunate enough to be forced to deal with.

'You just about ran him over,' Stuart Faison, the shotgun rider said as the stage rocked and skidded to a halt.

'Better see if there's any help for the man,' Dane said, and Faison nodded. Placing his shotgun aside in the coach box he clambered down heavily – for he was a large-built man – and approached the object in the road. The moonlight was clear and yellow, but the shadows along the pine-tree-lined road were deceiving. Stuart Faison approached the body, tipped back his hat and crouched down. Then he muttered a curse.

'It's only a log!' he called back to Dane Hoffman, who was having some trouble controlling the nervous four-horse team.

Someone had taken a log with projecting branches on it, dressed it in a white shirt and placed a hat over the end of the stump. Now why would anyone. . . ? Faison's innate caution caused rapid concern to rush from the back of his mind and he stood, reaching for his holstered handgun.

'You won't need that,' a voice said, and a man emerged from the pines, blue silk scarf across his face, hat tugged low. He carried a Henry repeating rifle at the ready. 'You'd better shed that gunbelt.'

'What is this, a hold-up?' Faison asked with mingled anger and astonishment. His livelihood depended on his ability to keep the stage from being looted. The man with the rifle, whoever he

6

was, answered with a touch of sarcasm.

'It sure looks that way, doesn't it? Drop that gunbelt before I'm forced to do something I don't want to do.' He took the rifle to his shoulder and aimed it squarely at Stuart Faison.

'All right, partner,' the big shotgun rider growled. 'I know when a man's got the upper hand.'

He unbuckled and dropped his gunbelt. Dane Hoffman sat on the box of the stagecoach with two thoughts in his mind. He could go for the shotgun beside him and try to stop this – assuming he did not hit Faison as well, and that was unlikely with a scattergun at this range. The second thought was that he was not going to be able to move more quickly than the highwayman could shift the sights of his rifle. He sat watching and waiting, frozen by fear and a healthy respect for the .44-.40 rifle the hold-up man was carrying. From inside the coach the self-important Mr Torrance yelled again.

'What's holding us up! I need to be at a meeting in Mesa at eight o'clock in the morning.'

'Now,' the highwayman was saying through his dark mask to Faison. 'I want you to start walking. Right up that ridge.' He indicated the direction he meant with his rifle barrel. 'Not into the trees, but straight up that cleared stretch.'

7

'How far do I. . . ?'

'Until I can't see you any more. Or until you think you're out of rifle range,' the hold-up man said, again with that nasty little bit of arrogance.

'The next time. . . .' Stuart Faison began threateningly.

'Get marching or you'll never have a chance at a next time,' the bandit said, and now his voice carried no humor. Faison began trudging toward the barren ridge upslope from the stage road. The highwayman watched him for a minute, then turned his attention to the coach.

'Better loop those reins and step down, driver,' he told Dane Hoffman. 'Toss that shotgun over the side! How many on board?'

'Just two. A man and his wife,' Dane said, twisting the reins to the team around the brake handle before climbing down to the moonlit road. The man with the rifle gestured him aside. 'Anything valuable in the boot?'

Inwardly Dane cringed. There was a small strongbox in the boot. Paper money being shipped from Tucson in exchange for gold. Enough to keep the banks in Mesa in business for another six months.

'Yeah,' he admitted reluctantly. What was the point in trying to deny it? 'About thirty thousand in paper, I think.'

'Suppose you unload that for me,' the highwayman suggested, and Dane started that way with a shrug. He told the robber:

'You know that they'll rescind those serial numbers. You won't be able to spend a dollar of it in the territory.'

'Is that the way it works? I didn't know that,' the man with the rifle said as he followed Dane to the rear of the coach. 'You're a knowledgeable man.'

'That's the way it's done – you see there are some advantages to the banks in preferring paper money over gold. You couldn't decline to honor gold, could you?'

'No,' the bandit agreed. 'I guess a man would have to spend this money fast or get out of the territory. But I guess it could be spent in Mexico, couldn't it?'

'I wouldn't know,' Dane said bitterly as he unstrapped the canvas covering on the boot and reached for the small strongbox there. 'I never lived an outlaw's life.'

'No? You'd be surprised what a man can be driven to. Just drop that strongbox and climb back aboard. If your friend's got half a brain, he'll cut down to the road on the other side of the hill and you can pick him up there.'

'All right. Look, mister,' Dane said, 'I'm telling you the truth: that is going to be hot money –

you'll never be able to spend it wherever you go.'

'That's all right,' the highwayman said amiably. 'I don't intend to try spending it.'

Dane hesitated. He was trying to study the man enough so that he might be able to identify him one day. He was tall, wide-shouldered, wearing a dark-blue shirt, dark jeans and had a blue silk scarf covering his face. That was all that Dane would be able to testify to with any certainty. The rifle in the highwayman's hands twitched again.

'I believe I asked you to clamber up into the box. I want to talk to your passengers for a minute. Then you can be on your way.'

Dane turned away and did as he was told. He did not wish to argue with the man. He had dealt with this sort in his time. You never knew when their mood might change and they would start shooting. It had happened before.

The highwayman stepped to the near door of the coach and swung it wide, backing away with his rifle in a ready position.

'Step out!' he commanded. The little man inside bent forward to peer out. The moon paled his face.

'What is this – a hold-up?'

'Looks like it,' the robber said. He repeated: 'Step out!'

'Tell him we refuse, Abel,' the woman beside

him urged, but Mr Abel Torrance instead slid from his seat to the ground. One never knew what these Western outlaws were capable of.

'You too, lady,' the highwayman ordered. 'Or should I shoot your husband to show you that I'm serious?'

The woman hesitated as if weighing Abel Torrance's life against her personal safety, but eventually she flounced down, skirt and petticoats billowing as she descended from the coach. Perhaps forty, she had dark hair that shone unnaturally in the moonlight, pinned tightly and topped by a tiny feathered hat.

Together the two weighed as much as a small pony. Whatever they did to make a living, food was no problem for them.

'Show me your wallet and empty out your pockets,' the robber ordered. He glanced toward the stagecoach box to make sure that the driver had not gotten any heroic ideas, and up toward the bare ridge to assure himself that Stuart Faison had not come up with any similarly reckless thought. The fat little man blustered.

'You have no right—'

'We're not talking about rights here,' the tall hold-up man replied. 'We're talking about who has the gun. Empty your pockets! Just drop it all on the ground. That'll be fine.' His eyes shifted to Abel

Torrance's chubby wife. 'You, lady, what have you got that I might find valuable?'

'My husband always carries our money. You might say he controls it all,' she said with acerbity. The two exchanged bitter glances. Trouble does not always bring out the best in people.

The highwayman noticed this silent exchange and watched as the round man emptied his pockets, throwing his wallet down as well, but his eyes lingered on the woman. The moonlight was silver now, revealing, and at the lobes of her ears dangled intricately made gold earrings with four diamonds in each. She seemed to sense his examination and she recoiled, placing the palms of her hands over her ears.

'Take them off,' the highwayman said.

'I will not!' she said stubbornly. 'They belonged to my great-aunt Estelle. Given to her by the King of Prussia.'

'Take them off,' the highwayman said again.

'I will not!'

'I'd hate to have to cut your ears off just to get them,' the robber said and even by moonlight it was clear that she blanched.

'Ruth!' her husband pled.

'Oh, all right!' the woman exclaimed, and she removed the earrings. She started to hurl them to the ground, but perhaps respecting their lineage,

12

she held out a trembling hand and the highway-man took them, putting them away in his shirt pocket.

'What's there?' the highwayman asked, looking at the pile of trinkets and bits of paper Abel Torrance had placed at his feet.

'Two hundred dollars expense money,' Torrance said sourly. 'The papers – they are my notes for the business meeting I have in the morning – if I get there. Of no value to anyone but me.'

'I'll keep those,' the hold-up man said and Abel Torrance showed fire for the first time.

'They're of no possible use to you! Take the money and be damned – I can have more wired to me in Mesa, but I need those notes.'

The highway man was not swayed, in fact he had ceased to listen to the rotund little man. His eyes had again fixed on an object that seemed to fasci-nate him. 'You're wearing a watch,' he said to Torrance. There was a gold chain across the man's vest, at the end of which, obviously, a watch should rest. 'Take it off.'

'That is my father's watch.'

'Is your father alive?'

'Not anymore. He—'

'Then it's not his; the dead own nothing. Now, I believe, it is mine. Unfasten it, drop it on the ground and climb back aboard the coach. I'm more than a little tired of your company.'

The watch dropped to the shadowed earth and gleamed coldly in the moonlight.

'Now,' the highwayman ordered roughly, 'get back on board. Driver! Whip those ponies out of here!'

'Just give me time. . . .' the woman complained, hitching up her skirts with one hand as she fumbled for the iron handhold. Abel Torrance, perhaps understanding the urgency of the situation better than she, shoved from behind and the woman toppled into the coach interior, Torrance scrambling after her as the sound of a bullwhip cracking past the horses' ears sent the animals into rapid, startled motion.

The highwayman was left alone in the night.

He let his eyes search the area, probing the shadows before he moved. Who knew? That shotgun rider might have decided to slink back, or there might have been some chance passer-by hidden in the trees. But nothing moved but the upper branches of the pines in the slight breeze, nothing sounded but the somewhat eerie voicing of a lone owl foraging for its midnight meal.

The highwayman returned to the copse where he had left his gray horse, led it back to the road and scooped up the articles he had taken from the

14

Torrances. These he stuffed into his saddle-bags, except for the diamond earrings which he still carried in his shirt pocket. The strongbox was a little more of a problem. Thankfully it contained only paper and not gold. Still, it was heavy enough to give him trouble before he managed to position it across his horse's withers.

Then with a final look around, the highwayman rode back the way he had come, through the scattered pine trees toward the pueblo of Tres Palmas.

Halfway along his route was the red stone bluff. Honeycombed with caves large and small, it had long been a hideout for men on the run. He, however, had no intention of sleeping here since he had his own bed at home and Margarita to share it with. He dropped the strongbox to the earth, swung down and carried it to one of the smaller caves, no more than six feet high and four wide, tall enough for a short man to enter without ducking.

There, in a dark corner of the nook, he placed the strongbox, emptied his saddle-bags of the other property belonging to the Torrances and removed the note he had penciled at home on the kitchen table. He spread it out on the top of the strongbox, weighted it down with the gold watch, and left, walking through the moon shadows toward his ground-hitched horse.

Swinging into the saddle he spoke. 'Come on, Poco, it's time to go home.'

The moon had begun to drop toward the far desert horizon. The shadows before the gray horse were long, crooked as it plodded on toward Tres Palmas. Its rider was suffering from brief remorse.

The earrings.

The ornate diamond earrings still rode in his shirt pocket. It was the first time he had kept any-thing from a robbery, and it was troubling him. He was not a thief, after all. But he had not liked that woman on the stage, and it seemed that, after all his work, he was due something in the way of payment. He did not want them for himself, cer-tainly. But Margarita went without many things these days. For a time she had been forced to take in washing. Their savings, such as they were, had long ago been spent. She hadn't had a new dress in years, and God knew that the woman deserved a small gift if he had little else left to offer. Thanks to Calvin Poole.

The lone rider's mouth tightened at the very thought of the hated name. Calvin Poole had brought all of this on himself. 'Well, Poole,' the highwayman thought, 'you're getting some of your own back now, aren't you?'

A few low-burning lamps glowed in the windows

16

of the small adobe houses ahead in Tres Palmas. They led the highwayman that way as the moon dimmed and fell to darkness.

# TWO

Marshal Patrick Donovan sat unhappily behind his desk in his Mesa, Arizona, office. The evening had started out badly and gotten worse. The Price brothers had decided to shoot up the Golden Eagle saloon around midnight for no particular reason that anyone knew of. Later still Clarissa Townshend had set fire to her little house on the edge of town, as she did periodically to frighten off the 'spirits'. A bucket brigade had put the fire out fairly quickly, and the house, being built of adobe block, had not suffered serious damage. No sooner had Donovan returned to the shelter of his room, rinsed the soot from his face and the blood from his knuckles and placed his head down on his pillow than the westbound Chicolote stage drew up before the office and a group of people swarmed toward the door, cursing, crying, shout-

18

ing and complaining at once.

Donovan knew two of the people – the stage-coach driver, Dane Hoffman and his shotgun man, Stu Faison. The other two were passengers: a portly red-faced gent in a town suit and his harri-dan wife who stood about six inches taller than her husband. They introduced themselves, when they eventually got around to it after shrieking and shouting complaints at the weary town marshal, as Mr and Mrs Torrance.

'Tell me again what happened,' Marshal Donovan said, his voice gravelly from yelling at the Price brothers, from inhaling smoke at Mother Townshend's house. 'One at a time, please!'

His guests were not in the mood to be orderly with their complaints. It didn't help any that Ben and Luke Price continued to yell from the back jail cell, demanding that they either be released or given whiskey.

'Man stopped us on the Fairmont Grade,' Dane Hoffman began excitedly. 'He had thrown a log across the road—'

'It looked like a man,' Stuart Faison interrupted, equally excited.

'Wait a minute,' Marshal Donovan said, holding up a hand. 'You said it was a man who stopped you. Are you now saying it could have been a woman?'

'I'm saying the log looked like a man,' Stu

Faison pressed on, surprised by the marshal's lack of comprehension. 'He had dressed the log up to resemble a man.'

'I see,' Donovan said wearily.

'Whiskey!' one of the Price brothers demanded. Donovan rose to close the door connecting the jail cells with the office.

'He took my father's watch!' the round little man, Torrance, complained loudly.

'Your father?' Donovan looked around the room. 'Where is he?'

'In his grave!' Torrance said.

Resting more comfortably than Patrick Donovan, the marshal hoped.

'He was rude,' the woman said, 'he nearly molested me.'

Donovan wasn't sure how someone could nearly be molested, but he let it pass. The woman was grinding her teeth. She had a horsy face, and the motion of her jaws only strengthened the resemblance.

'Did anyone get a good look at him?' Donovan wanted to know.

'He wore a mask, of course,' Ruth Torrance said, 'but he had evil eyes.'

Donovan pretended to write that down. Her description of the man would do a lot of good on a Wanted poster. Just then the door burst open again and Calvin Poole, owner of the Chicolote Stage Company tramped in, looking self-important. Behind the bulky Poole, two of the town's three bankers, both rumpled, tieless and out of breath, entered the room.

'What's this about another robbery?' Poole demanded, hooking his thumbs into his vest pockets. He rocked on his heels and stared accusingly at Donovan as if the town marshal were complicit in the matter.

'That's what I'm trying to find out now, Mr Poole,' Donovan answered tiredly.

'The currency?' one of the bankers, Howard Tibbits, asked with truculence.

'He got it, I'm afraid,' Dane Hoffman said.

'All of it?'

'It was all together, wasn't it?' Hoffman mumbled.

'You, Faison,' the stageline owner thundered. 'What do you think you were hired to do? How could you let a lone man stop the coach and hold you up.'

'We don't know if he was alone,' Stuart Faison said weakly. 'There could have been a gang hiding in the trees.'

'Was there?' Poole demanded.

'Just the one man,' Dane Hoffman said, trying to help out his shotgun guard. 'You see – there was

21

this log dressed up like a man in the road—'

'What do you intend to do about this, Marshal?' Poole asked angrily.

'What? What I always do – try to find the man and arrest him.'

'Well?'

'Well what?' Donovan asked, rapidly losing patience. He was tired and thirsty. He felt like getting the Price brothers a bottle of whiskey and sharing it with them. 'I need to know who I might be looking for and where he might be. That is what I'm attempting to do right now, and getting little enough help at it.'

'This is the second shipment of new currency that we've lost,' Howard Tibbits complained. No one but the other banker, Joe Thrush, commiserated with him.

'You got that shipment back,' the marshal reminded him.

'A stroke of luck. We can't expect that to happen again – and without paper money to circulate . . . we might as well go back to the days when all of the business in this town was transacted with pokes of gold-dust.'

The front door to the office opened again. Now what? Patrick Donovan thought, mentally cringing.

'*Señor?*' a cracked voice said warily. In the

doorway a local man, Pablo Martinez stood, straw hat in hand. He was emaciated, nearly toothless and blind in one eye. 'I have a thing for you, sir.'

Pablo approached the marshal's desk, proffering a sheet of yellow paper. Pat Donovan took it, glanced at it and then asked:

'Who gave this to you?'

'What is it?' Poole demanded to know.

'A message from the highwayman. Where did you get this, Pablo?'

Nervous now, the Mexican said, 'A man he give it to me. He give me fifty pesos to bring it to you.'

'Where is he?'

Pablo shrugged. 'He is gone.'

'When did he give it to you?' Donovan asked patiently.

'Earlier – this morning, you know. And fifty pesos. He say. . . .'

'Damn all that,' Calvin Poole bellowed. 'What did he look like, this man?'

'I don't know. I don't see too good from one eye, you know. He was pretty tall, taller than me.'

'Was he white, Mexican. . . ?'

'We've already established that he is white,' Donovan pointed out. 'A white man with evil eyes.'

'Let's forget all that for the moment,' Howard Tibbits put in. 'What does the note say, Marshal?'

'It just tells us where the loot is stashed,' Patrick

Donovan answered.

'Again!' Calvin Poole shouted. Pablo slipped toward the door as the Torrances and the two bankers crowded the marshal's desk even more closely.

'What does he mean "again"?' Abel Torrance wanted to know.

'The stage line has been robbed before,' Donovan told him, 'twice before. In each instance the robber has sent us word on where to recover the loot. He hasn't taken a cent as far as we know.'

'Then why. . . ?'

'I'll tell you why!' Calvin Poole fumed. 'He's out to destroy the Chicolote Stageline. He's driving my business off and scaring my passengers away.'

Howard Tibbits, the banker, was more pragmatic about affairs. 'Do you mean to tell me that the highwayman has informed you where the strongbox with the new currency can be found?' At Donovan's nod, he grew excited. 'Well, then, let's get moving!'

'Not in the dark,' Donovan said. 'We'd never find it. Come sunup I'll ride on down there. I know where it is – he even drew a little map,' Donovan added with a bent smile, holding the note up for all of them to see.

'Strange sort of man, this highwayman,' Abel Torrance commented.

24

'You all seem to think that no harm's been done,' the volatile Calvin Poole said bitterly. 'Well, you get your property back and you're content. Me – I've got to watch Chicolote's stock fall with each of these raids. People don't want to ship their goods on a line so prone to hold-ups. People don't want to ride our line. They don't feel safe; they don't think we're doing our best to protect them.' He shot a dark glance at Dane Hoffman and Stuart Faison.

'I'll tell you what, Donovan – either you catch this highwayman, and soon, or I'm bringing in someone who can. I've a man in mind.'

'I can't do more than I'm already doing,' Donovan said, feeling the beginning of a dull headache. 'I've an entire town to think of, not just you. But I caution you strongly against bringing in a hired gun, if that's what you have in mind. That sort of man carries trouble with him, and you know it.'

'I have a meeting at eight o'clock,' the practical and self-centered Abel Torrance said, putting his hat on. 'My wife and I shall retire to the nearest hotel. I wish the highwayman hadn't taken my notes with him, but I suppose it will all work out. I have a strong memory. So long as I get my father's watch back.'

'And my diamond earrings. Those were given to

my Aunt Estelle—'

'Yes, dear,' Abel Torrance interrupted. It was as firmly as he ever spoke to her. 'We know. Marshal, isn't it true that the Butterfield Stageline also has a terminus here in Mesa? We shall require passage east, and I doubt we will wish to travel on the Chicolote line again.'

'Anyone can tell you where their office is,' Donovan said as Calvin Poole reddened, seeming about to explode. He held back his remarks until the couple had left.

'You see, Donovan! That's what I mean. My company's getting a bad name. I don't imagine the banks or anyone else will wish to ship currency or anything of value on Chicolote until this is cleared up. I want that highwayman! I want his scalp, and I want it now!'

After Poole had stormed out, vowing vengeance, Stuart Faison and Dane Hoffman, both worried about the possibility of losing their jobs, left the marshal's office. The bankers had gone out in the middle of Calvin Poole's tirade, happier now that the stolen new currency they needed seemed to have been recovered.

Marshal Patrick Donovan remained at his desk, rubbing the heels of his hands against the bone above his eyes. He was in the wrong line of work, he decided. Decent men with decent jobs were home asleep now, next to their warm, chubby little wives. All he had to look forward to was five or six hours of sleep on his thin cot and a long ride to the Honeycomb in the morning.

He wanted the highwayman almost as badly as Calvin Poole did. But not out of any vengeful impulse. He just needed some rest, some peace of mind!

'We need whiskey!' one of the Price brothers shouted again, his voice sounding clearly through the oaken door separating the cells from Donovan's office.

They weren't the only ones, Patrick Donovan thought.


Mason Riddle was a truly evil man. He not only had evil eyes, but an evil mouth and two evil Colt revolvers, which he was prone to use at the drop of a hat, strapped to his hips. He was a bounty hunter by profession and a killer by nature. He saw nothing wrong in gunning a man down – sometimes mistakes were made, sure, but who was to say the man might not have gotten snake-bit the next day and died anyway?

Riddle figured that he just sort of moved things along.

He had accidentally killed a man when he was only thirteen years old. A man who had been raising hell in his hometown of Plainview, Kansas. The man had been bragging, shouting, had been stumbling drunk, and placed a hand on Riddle's mother. The man died and it later turned out that there was $500 reward money posted on him. That was more than his father and mother made in a year slaving against the stubborn clay of their dry farm.

It got Riddle to thinking that there were a lot easier ways to make a living than walking behind a plow six days a week.

Since then he had had a long and somewhat varied career – he shied away from publicity, believing it to be detrimental in his line of work. Therefore, although he was widely known in certain circles, the average man or woman would-n't have known him from Adam. All to the better.

He came, he did his job and was gone again with as little notoriety as possible, with his pockets fuller than they had been when he arrived.

Not tall, Riddle was very dark, possibly indi-cating some Mediterranean influence in his bloodline. Hairy arms, hairy chest, broad, bearded face, he nevertheless looked the same as many rough miners, buffalo skinners and trappers. His face would be memorable to a man only after he had no more use for the memory.

The job in Yuma was the sort he favored. The

law was on his side in this sort of work. Calvin Poole had made contact with him through mutual acquaintances of the hard sort, and offered $500 for the capture or killing of the unnamed 'Chicolote Highwayman' as the newspapers in Mesa now called him. Therefore, the job was reduced to finding the man, shooting him down and claiming the reward. Of course, Riddle had no intention of trying to capture the man alive. That could lead to all sorts of problems.

Shoot the man down and the situation was ended. If anyone ever asked for an explanation – few ever did, this being a rough country – a story could always be fabricated. There would be no one around to contradict Riddle's version of the incident.

It was, to Mason Riddle, money for nothing. Find the man who would not know who Riddle was, gun him down and take the reward with no more expense to him than the cost of a .44 cartridge.

First he had to find the man – that seemed to be the problem here. Riddle thought he had the easy answer to that. He meant to take a few rides aboard the Chicolote stage himself, especially when it made its run carrying valuables – Calvin Poole would know which those were. Then, when the highwayman made his try, he would find

Mason Riddle's guns there to answer him.

Finding no flaws in his plan of action, Riddle continued to ride his distinctive white horse with its gray mane and tail across the saguaro-stippled white sand desert toward Mesa.

'I cannot have this!' Margarita exclaimed, the English idiom escaping her. She was dark, beautifully slender, sloe-eyed. Just now she was looking at the diamond earrings that Hal Trevor had clumsily wrapped in a piece of red crêpe paper left over from a Christmas past. They glittered and gleamed in the sunlight of the new morning shining through the window of their small adobe house in Tres Palmas. 'They are too much, Hal, and we have so little to spend.'

'I found them,' Hal replied, hoping that his explanation sounded like a bashful admission. His wife shook her head seriously. Her eyes did not shine with disbelief, but doubt lingered in their depths.

'I don't think those are real diamonds anyway,' Hal Trevor continued, trying his best to appear as a shamed man who could only offer his woman found-trinkets. 'Probably they're only glass.'

'But they seem. . . .' Margarita, who had never owned a real diamond in her entire life, trembled between excitement and vague fear.

The fear was because her husband who had once worked steadily and stolidly to provide for them now had no apparent source of income, no seeming ambition.

And he was gone nights.

Frequently he would ride out of an evening and Margarita could only lie in bed, fearful, not knowing where her man had gone or when he would return. This time, as usual, she took the easy explanation as the truth.

'Well, they are beautiful anyway. The other women in town will be jealous,' she said as she went to the small oval mirror hanging on the wall and fastened the earrings on.

Hal Trevor watched with mingled pride and shame as the slender girl, the woman he loved, fixed them to her lobes, both appreciating his gift and doubting its provenance – he knew she did; she did not have to say it. Perhaps at times she even thought he was a common thief out there, lurking on the desert to waylay travelers. How could he explain?

There was no way, not without risking the loss of her love.

But he would not stop. Not until Calvin Poole was ruined. It had gone too far.

The young Spanish girl, the love of his life, turned from the mirror with the diamond earrings on her ears glittering in the sunlight. She spread her arms wide, offering him her comfort, and Hal Trevor went to her, for the moment not regretting the only mistake he had yet made in his war against the Chicolote Stage Company.

# THREE

'Damnit, Hal, you've gone too far,' Benson Trevor told his brother as the two men sat in front of the cantina, Tres Palmas's only saloon. Ben was drinking strong coffee, Hal sipping tequila. There was a thin tracing of shadow across the tiled patio from the wide-spreading thorny mesquite trees next to them. Of the three palm trees after which the settlement had been named, there was no sign. Either earlier settlers had sawn them down for unknown reasons, or they had simply died out over time.

'What do you mean, Ben?' Hal asked, using the moisture collected beneath his tequila glass to image a bit of scrollwork on the plank table's top.

'I mean those diamond earrings!' Ben said harshly but quietly, glancing around to see that he was not overheard. He clamped his thick hands

33

more tightly together and leaned forward, fore-arms on the table. 'Oh, yes, it's all very fine to tell Margarita that they're glass stones, but I saw them – and they are not glass! Others will see them and tell her the same thing. They're stolen goods, Hal! What were you thinking of?'

'She deserves something after these years of deprivation,' Hal said gloomily, staring into his half empty glass.

'Yes, she deserves something now – an honest man,' Ben replied. 'This all began with noble intentions, though some might think it reckless. But a man who becomes a thief is a thief.'

'The woman who had the earrings will never miss them,' Hal answered.

'How do you know that? Besides, this woman, whoever she was, has nothing to do with Calvin Poole and what he did to you.'

Hal didn't raise his head. He continued to brood; his brother's comments had struck a nerve. No, he supposed, the woman had not deserved to lose her diamond earrings. A vendetta once loosed can spin a wider loop than intended. Hal's only wish was to hurt Calvin Poole. To strike him where it would cause pain – in his pocket book, to drive the Chicolote Stage Line into the ground.

It had begun when Poole had first set eyes on Margarita, wearing her traditional off-the-shoulder white blouse and striped skirt in Mesa town. He had nudged Hal, then a temporary driver for the stage line and told him:

'I would like me some of that.'

Hal had stiffened and informed the coach line owner that Margarita was his wife, but Poole had forged ahead. 'Well, then, we need to do some bartering, don't we? A full-time job for a night with her.'

Hal had not hit Poole, not responded; he had simply walked off the job. The problem was, jobs were hard to come by in Arizona Territory then, and Hal had become a burden on Margarita, on her family and his friends. He lazed about, sulked and developed an abiding anger. He never told Margarita the reason for quitting his job, and she did not understand his moods.

One night as he lay awake with his woman at his side he made a decision – he would ruin Calvin Poole as Poole had destroyed his own life. It would be more satisfying than punching the fat-faced man in the jaw could ever have been. He had set out to destroy the Chicolote Line, and by all accounts had nearly succeeded. The banks were now chary of sending their currency on that particular line; travelers were beginning to show preference toward Butterfield, which had a far lower rate of hold-ups.

'It can't go on,' Ben Trevor was saying. 'It's time to pull the plug, Hal. You've done the man harm; now it's time for you to get yourself organized again. Find a real job and buy trinkets for Margarita with earned money. You have just turned the corner, brother. You've become nothing but a thief.'

'Because of one set of earrings?' Hal demanded savagely. His brother responded cautiously:

'Because of one set of earrings.' Ben stretched both hands forward and pleaded, 'Think about it, Hal. Perhaps what you were doing was noble in its beginnings, but you have stepped over the line. What's next? You decide to pop open one of those strongboxes and keep the contents?'

'Margarita deserves to have something,' Hal said, still angry at the truth his brother spoke.

'I know Margarita, not as well as you, perhaps, but if she knew where those earrings had come from, would she still wear them proudly around the pueblo?' Ben asked.

Hal Trevor did not answer. There was no answer. His thoughts, unreasonably or not, were fixed on the remark that his brother had made – one strongbox. Open one only. Thousands to buy a piece of land and stock it or make his way to Mexico where Margarita had family. Lately he had begun to think more of the profit to be made in

36

what he was doing than of his lust for revenge against Calvin Poole. It made him feel dirty and craftily optimistic at once.

It seemed to have all come about because of those damned diamond earrings.

Hal Trevor signaled the white-clad server for another glass of tequila and sat back, hands crossed on his stomach, pondering his life's future direction.

His name was Laredo, and he was hunting a man.

He did not know his name, where he lived, his face, but Laredo was looking. His career had started years before when he himself had been looking for a bank to rob.

His new path in life had begun because of a man named Jake Royle. Down and out on that desperate day, Laredo had been eyeballing the bank in a small town called Cannel in southern Arizona. Laredo was hungry, tired and broke. While he stood considering the bank, a man who moved on cat feet slipped up beside him in the hot shade of the alleyway and introduced himself.

'Jake Royle's my name,' he said, stuffing the bowl of a stubby pipe with tobacco.

'Pleased to meet you,' Laredo said shortly. He was not in the mood for idle conversation with a stranger.

'Working in town, are you?' Royle persisted, lighting his pipe.

'Not at the moment.'

Royle nodded, blew out a stream of blue smoke and studied the tall stranger. 'I, myself, am employed here,' he said. Laredo cast annoyed eyes on the stocky old-timer. 'For now, that is. I travel all around,' Royle continued, indicating all of the territory with a wave of his pipe.

'What are you, some kind of drummer?'

'No. I am employed, my young friend, as an operative in the enforcement arm of the Territorial Bank examiner's office.'

'Oh?' Laredo felt cornered suddenly. The inoffensive little man apparently had some standing. Laredo wondered how Royle could have known what he had in mind on that hot, dry morning.

'Yes,' Royle went on, 'you know men will try to stick up these little banks in isolated areas, and very often succeed. Then, once they have beaten the town marshal to the city limits, gotten out of the county before the sheriff can catch them, they figure they've gotten away with the job. They'll ride on to Mexico, California, anywhere, free as birds. Or so they think. The local law doesn't have the time or resources to expend on hunting them down. Me,' Royle said with a gnomelike smile. 'I've got all the time in the world, son. All the time in the world.' With that the little man nodded and walked away. Laredo stood watching. If that had not been a warning, it was the next thing to one.

It wasn't until late afternoon that Laredo traced Royle to the hotel room where he sat shirtless, bare feet propped up.

'Mr Royle,' Laredo said, 'how's chances of getting hired on in a job like yours?'

Now Laredo sat his buckskin horse and looked across the desert toward Mesa, Arizona. It had rained recently and a ground fog was rising with the heat of day, obscuring the line of mesas to the north. The landforms resembled a fleet of ships embarking on some mysterious mission, the illusion strengthened by the fog which was like a man might see arising at some Pacific port.

There was quarry ahead. Laredo had little to go on, no name, only a vague description, but the highwayman had disrupted bank business, and that made it Laredo's affair. Deacon Cody, Laredo's new boss – sporting a handlebar mustache, excitable and narrow, had dispatched him with only a shake of his head and a crooked smile.

'We have no idea who this guy is, Laredo. But I'm sure you can take care of it.'

God bless Cody for his optimism! There was nothing like hunting for an unknown man across

1,000 square of miles of empty land. Cody, a born detective, had considered the situation, though, and suggested:

'It has to be a disgruntled former employee. Someone who's basically honest – why else would he return the loot? You're looking for a very angry, probably dangerous man, Laredo. I know you can handle it.'

Again, thank God for optimists. Laredo was not so sure. A bleak land with a pale prospect spread out before him. He continued on his way, his buckskin horse laboring under him.

Wilbur Harrison was spindly to the extreme. He wore a straw hat on this heated day, and tugged idly at the sparse pale whiskers he believed were the start of a manly beard. Opposite him sat a woman he knew only as Mrs Martin, some relative of the storekeeper Martin, and beside him a man with more than his fair share of chin whiskers. Bulky, brawny, intimidating and smelly, he carried holstered twin Colt revolvers. Harrison tried to edge away from the man, but it was difficult in the close confines of the Chicolote stage.

In an odd and paradoxical way Wilbur felt reassured by the presence of the big, bearded man. He was traveling East searching for job opportunities which did not exist in this part of the country, and

40

had chosen Chicolote over Butterfield only because there rates were a few dollars lower – and Harrison had no money to spare. He knew well that there had been many hold-ups on this line. And so he took the occasional shouldering of the big man beside him with mingled disgust and a sense of security.

Wilbur had little enough to lose even if the Chicolote Highwayman did decide to halt their coach. There might have been two dollars in silver left in his purse – he hadn't dared to look. At home there was a girl of eighteen named Fortunata whom he badly wanted to marry, but her family – justly, it seemed, even if it was galling – had opposed the match, Wilbur being on the poor side of broke with no prospects ahead of him. And so he had scraped up a few dollars for this endeavor.

The stage jolted along as he peered out the window at the endless desert. The first stopping place, he knew, was a place called Flyburg. Not after the insect, but after a man named Julius Fly, long departed. Although, Wilbur – who had once ridden that far with some men who had convinced him that there was silver ore in the hills nearby – thought that either derivation for the town's name would have been apt.

Flyburg stank, it was dirty, but it was the only

place around for almost twenty miles that had a steady source of water. Which drew the insects. Mosquitoes, flies, cicadas, a swarming of crickets which did not move for a man but merely lay there to crunch underfoot, dragonflies and wasps all swarmed to Flyburg. Especially in the summer, which was now beginning.

None of that mattered. The stage never reached Flyburg.

At a snail's pace as the four horse team labored up the long, winding western grade of the Fairmont cut-off, with the sun low and red at their backs, the highwayman emerged from the dry stand of pines to flag the stage down. Wilbur heard the driver curse, the shotgun rider moan. Mrs Martin seemed on the verge of hysteria as the coach rocked to a halt. Wilbur glanced at the big man to his left and saw that he was smiling with quiet satisfaction.

Taken by surprise again, Stu Faison tossed down his shotgun and said to Dane Hoffman. 'This is the end of us, my friend.' For their jobs hung in the balance, and they had misplayed their cards once more. Calvin Poole would accept no more excuses.

Through the settling gray dust which trailed the coach as it swayed and braked to a stop, Hal Trevor approached once more, rifle in hand, blue silk bandanna across his face.

'Not you again!' Stuart Faison was unable to keep himself from complaining.

'Climb down, shotgun!' the Chicolote Highwayman commanded. 'You know the routine – start hiking!'

There was a moment during which Stu thought of arguing, doing something impulsive like rushing the man with the rifle, but while his likelihood of keeping his job after this new hold-up were thin to none, still he had zero opportunities for finding a new position if the highwayman gunned him down.

'I'm on my way,' he grumbled as he climbed down from the box.

'What are you carrying, driver?' Hal Trevor asked Hoffman. 'You might as well tell me,' he added reasonably. 'I'll find out anyway.'

'Gold dust to exchange for bank notes,' Dane Hoffman answered. He was even more depressed at his surrender than Faison. This was the end. He needed to find a new line of work.

'It goes both ways, doesn't it?' Hal Trevor said cheerfully. 'All right, let's have a look.'

They never got as far as the boot. Mason Riddle had slipped from his seat to the far side of the stagecoach. Before Hal had marched Dane Hoffman at gunpoint to the rear of the stage he had positioned himself behind one of the dusty jack pines beside the road. He gave no warning as he stepped out now and gunned Hal Trevor down, the echoes of his twin revolvers sounding long and far across the countryside.

'Enough of that bastard,' the big bearded man said savagely. Walking up to Hal he toed him with his boot, assuring himself that the highwayman was dead. Then he began to have second thoughts.

There was a $500 reward for the hold-up man. But how much in gold was this coach carrying? Certainly more than that. Mason Riddle had never claimed to be an honest man. It was doubtful that he knew the meaning of the word.

'Thanks, partner!' Dane Hoffman said, his gratitude effusive. He thrust out a hand toward Riddle, but the big man refused it.

'How much gold do you reckon is in that boot?' he asked coldly.

'He had us cut the horses out of their traces,' Dane Hoffman was saying to the marshal, 'and then he made off with them, riding one, another one carrying the strongbox; the others naturally herded along. We were stuck good and proper.'

'Walking back toward Mesa, we were,' Stuart Faison put in, 'with that woman, Mrs Martin crying all the way. If the westbound stage hadn't happened by and picked us up, we'd still be walking.'

'But the hold-up artist, the so-called Chicolote Highwayman he was killed?' Marshal Pat Donovan asked.

'Yes, sir, he was shot down by the passenger . . . whatever his name was.'

'Mason Riddle,' Calvin Poole managed to unclench his jaw enough to say.

'Then, like I told you, he took off with the bank gold,' Faison concluded.

'What did he look like – this Mason Riddle?'

'He had a bushy black beard,' Dane Hoffman said.

'That doesn't narrow it down much. Anything else?'

The stagecoach driver looked to Stu Faison, who offered no help, then he shrugged. 'That's the only way I can describe him,' Hoffman answered.

'All right,' Marshal Donovan said wearily. He had had enough of all this business. 'This Mason Riddle, he's a man you hired, Mr Poole?'

'Yes,' Poole admitted as if it pained him. 'He was supposed to bring down the highwayman, since my regular employees seemed incapable of doing that.' He shot one more menacing glance at Dana Hoffman and Stu Faison. They both knew that they were through now. Poole would fire them the moment this interview was over. Faison, for one, felt termination was justified. He had let the stageline down, no doubt about that.

'Then the highwayman is dead – does anyone know him? Where's the body?'

'Still up on the Fairmont Grade,' Hoffman said. 'What were we to do, lug him in over our shoulders?'

'No,' the marshal said, groaning inwardly. That meant that he was going to have to ride out to the Fairmont cut-off tomorrow. 'Did you recognize him?'

'Yes, sir, he used to be a part-time driver for us. It was a man named Hal Trevor. We both knew him.'

'The man was trouble,' Calvin Poole growled.

'Well, he won't be anymore,' Donovan said, tilting back in his chair, placing clasped hands behind his head. 'The thing is, now what about this Mason Riddle? It seems that he's taken over the patch, doesn't it?'

'Fox in the henhouse,' Calvin Poole said bitterly.

'What's that?'

'I say I put a fox in the henhouse to guard the chickens,' Poole said with savage heat.

'So it seems,' Donovan answered carefully. 'Do you think he'll clear out now? You know him, Mr Poole, no one else does.'

'I *don't* know him!' Poole said. 'He was recommended to me by certain people. I was told he was

46

capable of a job like this.' The look he gave Pat Donavan intimated that the marshal was anything but capable in his work. Donovan frowned, understanding, but he got in his barb.

'It seems he was overqualified,' the marshal said.

'Are you going after him?' Poole demanded.

'Which way did he go, boys?' the marshal asked the stage driver and shotgun rider.

'How would we know? He was frisky with those guns is all we know – we weren't going to hang around to find out where he was going.'

Poole could take no more. 'You're both fired, you know?'

Stu Faison answered for both of them. 'We figured as much.'

Calvin Poole glared at the town marshal as if wishing he had the authority to fire him as well, but he knew that the truth was that Donovan could do virtually nothing now unless Riddle was stupid enough to show up in Mesa again.

After a few meaningless words of parting, Calvin Poole stepped out into the desert night to watch the stars, listen to the uproar at the always boisterous Golden Eagle saloon, curse his fate and start away.

He nearly walked into the tall man.

The stranger had white alkali dust on his blue jeans, faded blue shirt, face and fawn-colored

47

Stetson hat. He smiled, showing good teeth and spoke quietly to Calvin Poole.

'I hear you might be looking for someone to manage security on your stageline,' Laredo said.

# FOUR

Ben Trevor sat in front of the cantina in a black mood as night began to fall. Margarita was inconsolable. Ben had known it was going to happen, had tried to warn his brother, but it had been to no avail. Hal was dead, gunned down on the Fairmont cut-off. What had happened there he could not guess, but it had been inevitable, and now a young widow lay crying in her bed. Worse, Margarita had confided in him the day before that she was carrying his brother's child.

Damn all! Why hadn't Hal been able to stop his nearly addictive hatred for the Chicolote Line and its owner, Calvin Poole? None of it any longer made sense. Hal could have found some other kind of labor, anything, and been home tonight with his lovely little bride. But, no, Hal would have his revenge.

It all made Ben Trevor sick. He shook his head as the waiter approached him and rose to stretch and wander off down the deserted main street of Tres Palmas. Going. . . ? He suddenly realized he had no idea where he was going. The sky was star-bright but Ben Trevor walked along, boots raising tiny puffs of white dust, as if under a dark cloud.

Margarita.

Ben realized that he had always loved the girl, but after she had chosen to marry Hal, he had managed to banish thoughts of having her from his mind. Now he loved her still, but it was a different sort of caring. The woman was widowed, expecting a child, and soon would not be able to do the extra work needed just to survive. Ben felt that he owed her something, as he owed something to his brother's memory.

But what was there to do? Ride into Mesa and shoot down Calvin Poole who had been the cause of this? What would that solve?

Or continue down the very path he had urged his brother not to follow? Ben halted in his tracks next to the general store. A late delivery wagon rumbled past. The men who had found Hal Trevor's body up along the Fairmont cut-off where they had gone to load firewood for the people of Tres Palmas were distant cousins of Margarita.

Along with Hal's body they had brought in Poco, his little sorrel pony with the white diamond on its nose.

A man riding Poco, masked and concealed by night shadows, could be easily mistaken for Hal Trevor. A ghost mysteriously returned to haunt the Chicolote Stageline.

Once would do it. Once when the stage was carrying westbound currency, or eastbound gold to pay for it. One stick-up, only one, would support Margarita and her unborn child for years. And it would trouble Calvin Poole forever, puzzle him since he assumed that Hal was dead – wondering when the ghost of Hal Trevor might return again. But it had to be once.

Only once, Ben Trevor reminded himself. For he was no more of a thief than his brother had been.

Once only. He walked on feeling as if a burden had been lifted from him. It was hardly a crime; it was due justice for the family of a man Calvin Poole had driven to his grave.

*That was easy*, Mason Riddle was thinking as he crouched over his small campfire, counting the gold coins that glittered and gleamed in the flickering light. Nothing to it. He wasn't good at counting, nor at estimating, but as near as he could reckon, he was sitting with $20,000 in small gold-dust spread across his blanket. The dust was in small vials, which the banks used for measuring and totaling their value.

That could last a careful man a long time. Not five years previously Riddle had briefly worked as a cowhand before he had let a grudge against the ranch owner develop into a killing mood. Then he had been paid a dollar a day. Calvin tried to figure out how long it would have taken him to accumulate $20,000, but gave it up. The thinking was not worth the trouble.

But – he pondered – why settle for what he had already taken? Everyone knew that the Chicolote Line was easy pickings. Who would stop a man from holding it up again? Not that do-nothing marshal in Mesa.

Maybe, he thought with grim amusement, he could continue the myth of the Chicolote Highwayman – that way there would be no connection to him. If that was what it took, he could even shave his beard. Wearing a mask in the dark, no one would know the difference. The idea was both amusing and fascinating to Riddle.

Blaming it all on a dead man.

Only one more robbery would set him up for life. Hell, all he would be sacrificing was a few whiskers which probably were due for a shave anyway. It was something to ponder. Riddle kicked sand over his fire to put it out, tucked the stolen gold into his saddle-bags and rolled up in his blanket to catch some sleep while a restless pack of desert coyote pups yipped in the distance.

Wilbur Harrison was more than pleased with the way things had worked out, although it seemed he was the only one. His mother had quoted an old saying – how did it go? – something like 'It's an ill wind that blows nobody good.' He couldn't remember exactly. The trip East to look for work had been aborted by the stagecoach hold-up, but Calvin Poole, losing his temper, had found himself in need of a driver after firing Dane Hoffman. Wilbur figured he had little experience, but believed that he could handle a four-horse team. And all of the horses on the Chicolote Line knew their route.

Now, suddenly, he was not only unexpectedly employed, but closer to home and to his Fortunata, whom he still had strong intentions of marrying. She, sleek if slightly chubby, had been thrilled when, at the prospect of having a steady job at a fair income, Wilbur told her of the development.

Allaying Wilbur's uneasiness about driving the notedly dangerous run, was the hiring by Calvin

Poole of a competent-looking guard known to Wilbur only as 'Laredo'. It was sort of hard to define Laredo. His face was almost hawkish, but his mouth was pliant, and for all of his apparent toughness, the man smiled easily. He was a good man to have on your side, Wilbur decided.

Laredo rode the stagecoach box with both eyes open, rifle propped up between his legs. The new young driver fumbled a bit and whipped the horses at times when there was no real need to, but none of that concerned Laredo. He was on the job and guarding another $10,000 in gold that the bankers, Howard Tibbits, Joe Thrush and a third man whose name escaped him had packaged together to exchange for much-needed paper currency.

Calvin Poole had been reluctant to take Laredo on, but after they had held a meeting with the town bankers and Laredo had showed them his credentials, the owner of the stage line had been overruled. It wasn't the way Laredo usually chose to go about his work. He preferred to remain anonymously in the shadows, for although few men knew him on sight, his name and reputation were well known to those who made their living on the wrong side of the law. What he was dealing with here was a little different. All of them had concluded that the unknown stage hold-up artist was a disgruntled former employee. Meaning he was an amateur and could not know of Laredo's reputation, even if he were alive, which seemed unlikely. Hal Trevor's body had not been found, but it seemed clear that Mason Riddle had plugged him with enough lead to do the job.

Still Laredo did not like having his presence known publicly. People always talked.

Once not too long ago, word of Laredo's arrival had leaked out and he had been ambushed on the streets of Scottsdale by a gang of men he had been pursuing. That shoot-out had caused him to spend five weeks in bed recuperating. He was not eager to repeat the experience.

Especially now after he had met, wooed and wed that funny little Irish girl, Dusty, while on assignment in Crater, Arizona. Dusty had not wanted him to continue working for the bank examiner's office, but she knew Laredo to be an unsettled man, and realized that he could not sit alone on the front porch just because it was safer there.

Jake Royle had retired at last a few months back, but the new chief of the enforcement arm, Deacon Cody, was just as insistent that Laredo continue on the payroll. Dusty had inherited quite a bit of money; they really did not need the work, but

Dusty recognized that Laredo did need the excitement that his dangerous job provided. She was not sure she understood it, but she accepted it as a fact, a part of her man's character.

'Because it is the Territorial Bank examiner's business,' Laredo had said shortly when at the meeting the Chicolote Stage Line owner had expressed doubts about Laredo – a man he did not know – riding guard for his shipments.

'It's true,' little Howard Tibbits said, wiping the lenses of his spectacles on a cloth.

'We have the most to lose here, Calvin,' Joe Thrush chipped in, leaning forward excitedly in his chair. 'It's our gold going East, it's our paper currency coming West that is being taken.'

'*Was* being taken,' the heavyset Poole said sourly. 'The robber was killed, remember?'

'Did Marshal Donovan find the body?' Tibbits asked.

'No – you know he didn't,' Poole snapped back, his tone implying that Donovan couldn't find the boots on his own feet on a good day.

'Then we don't even know if the highwayman is really dead,' Thrush said, his face intense. 'Perhaps he was just knocked out, wounded. We don't even know if it was a single highwayman or a gang.'

'It was only the one man,' Poole said, obviously

tired of going over the subject. 'Hal Trevor. He always operated the same way. Hiding out the loot, then sending some kid or some local idiot to the marshal's office with a note telling us where to find it. And he always left a personal note to me.'

'What did the last one say, Calvin?'

'I don't use that kind of language,' Poole replied stiffly.

'But all of the loot was returned?' Tibbits asked.

'You know that it was,' Poole said with deepening impatience, 'you got your currency didn't you? Everything was returned, down to Abel Torrance's gold watch which was used to weigh down the note. The only thing we couldn't find is a pair of diamond earrings belonging to Mrs Torrance.'

Laredo stirred, uncrossing his long legs, frowning just a bit with his eyebrows.

'What are you thinking?' Tibbits asked.

'He's got a woman – or had one, if he's dead. A man wouldn't lift that single item for himself to sell, not with all the cash so readily available.'

'So he's got a woman!' Poole exploded, spreading his arms in a wild gesture.

'So she's probably wearing those earrings,' Joe Thrush, who was married, said. 'He didn't give them to her, and then say "Here I stole these for you. Hide them away so that no one ever sees them".'

'That might be a help sometime in the future – if we ever happen to run across the woman – but for now what are we going to do?' Poole wanted to know.

'I'll be riding your line for a while. Back and forth between here and Tucson. If you don't want to hire me, I'll pay my own way.'

'We'll pay his fare if that's what you want, Calvin,' Thrush said. 'Personally I don't understand your reluctance. It's your passengers and your line that Laredo is here to protect.'

That was the way it went on for another troubling half-hour. Laredo also wondered why Poole, knowing who Laredo was, was reluctant to let him ride. Perhaps the man just enjoyed what power he had even to the point of self-defeating obstinacy. No matter, Laredo would not be denied – he would have gone along even if it meant trailing the stage on his horse. Everyone believed – or hoped – that this business was over. Laredo meant to be sure.

One of his first moves when they did reach Tucson was going to be to march into Deacon Cody's office and tell him that the banks had better consider shelling out a few bucks to provide better security for these small coach lines if they were going to be shipping gold and currency on them.

Butterfield, Laredo knew, would have hired extra outriders after the first hold-up; it had its reputation to consider. Of course, the large line had more resources than a man like Poole.

Now, riding beside young Wilbur Harrison, he let his eyes search the long desert and the Fairmont Grade approaching, where scattered pines guarded the winding mountain ascent. Harrison, who had been driving well enough, if not as fluently as a more practised man, now appeared noticeably tense. His hands moved a little uncertainly, sometimes confusing the off-wheel lead horse, a strapping bay which glanced back and seemed to want to say, 'I know the way!'

'Take it easy, Harrison,' Laredo said in a quiet, firm voice. He smiled when Wilbur looked his way, his hat brim folded back by the wind, his hands sheathed in fringed gauntlets. 'You're doing fine.'

'Not too bad for my first run, huh?' Wilbur tried for a smile too, but it was almost a sickly expression. He said with concern, 'They probably got that highwayman anyway, didn't they?'

'That's what everyone says. I wasn't there,' Laredo answered.

'Yeah . . . probably got him. Riddle, he opened up with both pistols.'

'Then took the gold himself.'

'That's what he did, yes. He's probably ridden far away, too, wouldn't you think? He had himself a good pay-day.'

'That's probably what he did,' Laredo agreed. It did nothing to calm the young man's nerves, however, as they started up the long dusty grade into the scattered pine forest, Wilbur's face grew even more tense, his hands more uncertain on the eight reins he held spaced between his fingers. Laredo was just about to offer to spell Wilbur because the horses were angry; you could tell that. The messages they were getting were contrary – 'left, right, stop, slow down, hurry up.'

Entering the forest Laredo took his attention away from the driver to fix it on the surrounding trees where a man – men – could be hidden. The coach on this run carried no passengers, there being few willing to choose Chicolote over Butterfield these days, but it did carry a small strongbox with bagged gold-dust from the upper Gila River country. Would a bandit know that? Maybe: the miners would have been congratulating themselves in Mesa, drinking and probably all too eager to tell how they had struck it rich.

Other thieves would not be so sly. Taking a stage, after all, was mostly a hit or miss proposition anyway. If there was nothing worth taking aboard this one, there would be another along in a few days.

'It was just along this stretch of the grade that he. . . .' Wilbur Harrison was saying when the highwayman stepped out from the heated shade of the pine trees and leveled his rifle in their direction.

'It's him!' Wilbur Harrison shouted as the masked man stepped to the middle of the road. Reflexively he was pulling the team to a halt. Laredo shouted at him.

'For God's sake, man, don't stop!'

Wilbur was not sure what to do. The horses were not sure what to do. As Laredo slipped over the side of the box and found the step rung with his boot toe, intending to slide through to the other side of the coach, the team bolted.

Laredo lost his long gun as he was jerked forward. As he groped for the sill of the window the door flung itself open and Laredo was suspended from it as the coach lurched forward through the pines. Abruptly Harrison applied the brake and reined the team in, sending them nearly to their haunches, then the door jerked the other way, slamming itself shut. Laredo's only choice was to drop to the ground, and so he half-stumbled, half-fell to the dry earth, drawing his Colt revolver. Thank God he had not lost that.

There was a thick cloud of fine gray dust in the air still. The horses were pawing at the earth, turning one way and then the other in confusion.

If Harrison had control of the team, it wasn't apparent. As Laredo circled to the rear of the coach, moving in a crouch, the team, despite the brake being set, backed the coach into him.

Still using the coach as a shield, Laredo peered around the stage and caught a glimpse of the masked man to his left. Laredo raised his Colt and triggered off a round. The shot had been meant only as a warning at that distance, but it seemed to strike too near to the highwayman for his liking, and as Laredo watched, he turned and bolted back into the trees. In another minute Laredo saw the fleet shadow of a horse running from the pines, beelining it south towards white desert, in the general direction of Tres Palmas. There was no point in shooting again; at this distance it would be like hurling stones after the bandit.

Laredo holstered his pistol, surprised to find that his hand was trembling. He made his way back through the thin dust of the roadway to where his rifle lay, and scooped it up. He was perspiring heavily now, for the day had grown hot and his eyes stung with the dust, but he made his way quickly back to where the coach rested behind a trembling team.

'We did it!' Wilbur Harrison exulted as Laredo approached. 'Ran that highwayman off!'

Laredo did not respond to the boy's enthusiasm

except to offer, 'Would you like me to drive for a while?'

'That was some excitement, I'll tell you,' Wilbur went on as Laredo clambered aboard again. 'Wait until I tell Fortunata about it! She's the girl I'm engaged to. Are you married, Laredo?'

'Just recently.'

'Is it a big change in a man's life? I mean. . . ?'

'It's a big change,' Laredo said, watching the road as Wilbur continued to drive.

'I'm surprised your wife lets you do what you do,' Wilbur commented.

'She doesn't like it much.' No, Dusty didn't like it. It was always in her eyes to say something, but she never did. 'But it's what I do. I don't suppose there's a single lawman alive whose woman doesn't worry about her man living constantly at risk.'

'No. That's what I was thinking,' Wilbur said as he drifted the coach into a rut and let it jolt through it. 'I want to tell Fortunata all about this, but I'm afraid she'll decide that this job is too dangerous for me.'

*Maybe it is, the way you drive,* Laredo thought but did not say.

Wilbur Harrison went on chatting away about Fortunata and his prospects, relaxing after a little while. They had ridden on for nearly ten minutes more before the highwayman appeared in the road.

'Pull up that team and toss down your guns,' the masked man commanded.

# FIVE

'Pull up that team and throw down your guns,' Mason Riddle had shouted, but the men in the coach box did neither. To his surprise the driver snapped his reins and the horses bolted ahead at a dead run. Riddle had to fling himself aside to avoid getting run down. He got angrily to one knee and fired at the coach, but the man riding guard fired first and was more accurate.

Laredo's rifle bullet ripped through Riddle's shoulder near the collarbone, slamming him back. Riddle howled with fury and pain, rose enough to fire three more shaky shots at the stage, all of which flew wildly off into the trees. In pain, his temper simmering, it was a long while before Riddle could rise to his feet. By then there was nothing left to be seen but the thin tracing of light dust hanging along the tree-lined road.

'Was that better?' Wilbur Harrison panted as he slowed the team slightly to take a wide outside bend along the cliff beside the down hill extension of the cut-off.

'Much,' Laredo told the young driver. 'Of course, if we'd had passengers aboard, we would have had to play it different.'

'I understand,' Wilbur said. It was obvious that the kid was trying to learn, and he seemed eager to impress Laredo as well. The first was important, the second made no difference. 'Did you get him?' Wilbur wanted to know.

'I'm pretty sure I nicked him, but the way he was scrambling around, trying to get away from the horses, I didn't have a real good shot at him.'

Wilbur's grin expanded. 'He was scrambling, wasn't he. Man! I never thought of a team of horses as a weapon before, but they sure worked. Laredo,' he asked, 'was that the same man, do you think? Or another one. Is it a gang after all?'

'I'm pretty sure it was a different man – this one seemed to be more wide-built, though I never got a good look at the first one back there. As to if it's a gang, I just don't know. Everyone told me it was just one man – this Hal Trevor – but they never did find his body. So is he dead or not? Was that one man back there, or two? Is it some ghost of Trevor that we're going to have to pass by for ever as he keeps haunting the Chicolote?'

Laredo was only being fanciful, but Wilbur Harrison seemed to consider the idea soberly. The ghost of a dead highwayman forever returning to haunt the stage line. . . . They began rolling down the eastern grade towards Flyburg, their first stop, and Harrison put his mind back on handling the horses along this tricky stretch of Fairmont Grade.

*That was it! That was close enough,* Ben Trevor was thinking as he guided his brother's horse, Poco, across the white sand desert towards Tres Palmas. He didn't have what it took to be a robber. The guard on board the coach had missed him with a wild shot, but what if he hadn't? Today, Ben realized, could have been the last day of his life. And what would that do to aid Margarita when she needed him? Nothing.

He determined to find another job as soon as possible. Two, perhaps. He would work seven days a week from sunup to sundown if need be, and he would make sure that Margarita would have enough food and clothes for herself and the new baby when it came. One day, maybe, after the child was born, Ben could ask her the question he had wanted to ask her for so long. The question he would never have been able to ask if he had been shot down trying to rob that stagecoach.

'Poco,' Ben said stroking the sorrel's neck so that it turned its ears to listen to him, 'it is better, I think, to be a live poor man than a rich dead one.'

The whiskey was running low and so was the stack of silver dollars on the table between Stu Faison and Dane Hoffman as they sat in the Golden Eagle saloon on this hot, hopeless day.

'I told you what we should do,' the big man, Faison, was saying.

'It's whiskey talk, Stuart!' the stage driver answered, miserably turning his glass in small circles, staring into the amber liquor. 'We're done in Mesa, we'd just as well ramble.'

'I think I'm right,' Faison insisted, leaning forward, eyes intent. 'If anyone should know how to do it, it's us.'

'Rob your own employer?' Hoffman said. 'It's shameful.'

'He's not our employer,' Faison said powerfully. He reached across the table to grip Dane Hoffinan's wrist. 'He fired us, remember?'

'Yes, but—'

'Don't you see,' Faison interrupted, 'no one would ever suspect us. Plus, we can always find out when a stage with gold is leaving. All we have to do is hang around the station with our old friends, as if we were hoping that Poole might take us back.'

'I don't like it.' Hoffman took a drink of raw whiskey. Was the liquor here getting worse, or had he lost his taste for it? Probably that half-breed who worked in the saloon was making it in a barrel out back.

'I don't like it either,' Faison said. 'But I like going out into the world dead broke a lot less. Don't tell me you'd feel sorry for Calvin Poole.'

'I hate the lousy bastard!' Hoffman said with extreme vehemence. 'That's not to say I want to become a highwayman because of him.'

'It's a snap; why, if we needed to we could snatch the entire coach at a water stop like Flyburg. Unless you've suddenly forgotten how to drive.'

'I don't like that idea,' Dane Hoffman said, lifting his red eyes to stare at his friend. 'But that trick of a log across the road wasn't bad.'

'No it wasn't,' Faison said, gaining enthusiasm. 'And there's no need to dress it up like the high-wayman did to us – that's getting too fancy. If there's a log in the road, someone has to get down and move it – whoever's riding shotgun. And there's no way a man can do that and hold a gun at the same time.'

Dane still didn't like the idea, but as the whiskey settled his mind warmed to the possibility – just the possibility. It was something to consider.

'How much money do we have left between us, Stu?'

'There it sits,' Faison answered, flicking a finger at the silver coins on the table. 'Looks like three dollars to me.'

'I mean in the world.'

'Same answer.'

Dane Hoffman nodded. 'I'll tell you what,' he said, emptying his glass. 'Let's get us two more shots of whiskey and give the matter some serious thought.'


'I hear you got him,' Deacon Cody said eagerly. It was odd to see the younger man sitting behind Jake Royle's old desk. The two were completely different: Royle had been placidly confident and built like a rubber ball. Deacon Cody was thin and energetic, always moving, twisting the tips of his handlebar mustaches. The two had one trait in common, however. Both were intense about their job. Royle always used to have his boots off behind the desk, Laredo thought that Deacon Cody might be the kind of man who slept in his.

'I winged a second highwayman today,' Laredo replied, balancing his fawn-colored hat on his crossed knee. 'The first one was gunned down by a man Calvin Poole hired. The third one got away clean.'

'How many are there!' Cody asked, obviously surprised.

'Let's say three. But I think that two of them were only trying to pretend to be the dead man,' Laredo explained.

'Why?'

Laredo shrugged. 'Reasons of their own, maybe trying to lay the blame on someone who's no longer around to pay for the crimes.'

'Using the dead man as a disguise?'

'That's the way I read it. Of course,' Laredo said, recrossing his knees and repositioning his hat, 'I could be wrong. There's some talk that this is a gang of men doing the work, although no one's ever seen more than one at a time.'

'Could they be tracked?' Cody asked thoughtfully as he fidgeted with his mustache.

'It's hard country. A shale slope down from the grade and then white sand beyond. Neither takes prints well, as you know. The man I saw escape was riding hard south – there's nothing that way for fifty miles but a little pueblo named Tres Palmas. I think that was where he was going. I mean, he'd have to come from somewhere near by to even know the stage line was there, let alone hope to hit it and return to his hideout quickly.'

'I suppose that's so.' Deacon Cody grew meditative, and for him that meant rising to pace the room where a faded map of Arizona Territory hung on one wall, a lithograph of migrating Plains Indians on another. 'Is there any point in going down to Tres Palmas and asking questions?'

'I doubt it.'

'Is the local law being much help to you?' Cody wanted to know.

'Marshal Pat Donovan is a congenial man,' Laredo said, letting Cody draw his own conclusions. When Cody eventually returned to his unpadded swivel-chair, Laredo said, 'What needs to be done is to hire outriders for these coaches when they are carrying gold or currency. You must know some good men, Deacon. The banks can well afford to pay them.'

'Yes, yes you're right of course. If we're dealing with a single highwayman – or a string of them – one or two men riding guard should be enough to protect the bank's money. I'll propose that to the bank commission immediately.'

Cody had risen again and Laredo took that as his cue to rise also.

'Laredo, it's all well and good to lay future plans for protection, and I see no problem in arranging that. But I want those highwaymen. They need to be taught a lesson and held up as examples to other would-be robbers, and you're the only one who can track them down for me.'

'Am I?' Laredo asked with a thin smile.

'I know that you can handle it,' Deacon Cody answered, stretching out a bony hand.

Again, that far-reaching confidence. Laredo only nodded, shook Cody's hand and positioned his hat on his head.

'One thing, Deacon, I will want a month off work after this is finished. Dusty will want to know that she still has a husband.'

Thinking still of his Dusty, Laredo returned to his hotel room, asked for paper, pen and ink and sat down to write her a letter. It was always difficult to do: no matter how much was happening, it was hard to explain in a way she would understand, without her knowing all of the background. He decided to save all that for another time when they could sit at the kitchen table over morning coffee and discuss his time away from her. For the time being he decided to write only that he was going to take a month off after he had completed this job, and added the shortest, most common PS in the language.

Mason Riddle was fuming. Flat on his back, he stared up at the rough wooden ceiling of the adobe house. He had been a gunman most of his adult life, but this was the first time he had truly been shot. Oh, men had come close – that was what had happened to the tip of his little finger. But this time that Winchester slug the stagecoach guard cut loose had gotten him good and proper in the upper chest right where his left arm was jointed into it.

It hurt like blazes. It throbbed and burned and ached – so did his head, for that matter. Riddle had taken a lot of self-medication, tequila, before he had allowed some local medicine woman to treat him. He lay there cursing, hoping that he wasn't going to lose that arm, hoping that his head would do him a favor and just roll off his shoulders to the floor.

The medicine woman – it was stretching it too far to call the shriveled-up old Mexican woman a doctor – had told him that the town was called Tres Palmas. And that was where he now lay sweltering in the noonday desert heat, his head aching, his arm cinched tight. To top it off his cheeks and throat itched horribly. Having decided to take off his beard to resemble the Chicolote highwayman more closely, he had done the job without the help of soap or a barber.

He would not forget this.

He would get his own back – from Calvin Poole, from the stagecoach line, from that spindly driver who had tried to run him down, and especially from that guard with the rifle. He would remember that one's face. Riddle had gold stashed that he could recover and make his way out of the territory, but he felt a blood obligation was due.

When he was stronger he would return and he would take his vengeance on all of them, even if he had to hunt them down one by one and burn every coach, the stage station itself, and slaughter every one of their horses. He was that mad, and he didn't think his mood would change when he was well again. It never occurred to Riddle that all of this was his own fault.

Laredo had nothing against an extra day's rest, but it was somehow frustrating. He wanted to finish this assignment and get home. The currency bound for Mesa had been delayed in shipping and today's coach was running without valuables, but carrying five passengers who could not be put off for another day.

The horses would be rested for another twenty-four hours, and since the line, like many others, wished to keep the same driver with individual teams to breed familiarity, Wilbur Harrison was being replaced by an old-time rough and wooly man named Bert DeFord. The young coach driver was delighted by the opportunity to visit the new and much larger town of Tucson, but he had told Laredo:

'You don't have to stay around just to take care of me, Laredo. I know you want to get back on the line.'

'I do,' Laredo had replied, 'but after all, protecting those passengers is not my obligation. I work for the banks, and my first duty is to guard their currency. So, do what you like, Wilbur. Me, I'm just going to stretch out on my bed and catch up on some sleep.'

So it was that Laredo and Wilbur Harrison both enjoyed their leisure (though in vastly different ways) in Tucson while Bert DeFord, with a savage-looking man named Patterson, only recently hired, riding shotgun, lined out towards the distant terminus by way of the now infamous Fairmont cut-off.

The day seemed to trickle by. There was blowing dust. The pine-tree scent was dry and nearly over-powering as Dane Hoffman and Stuart Faison sat hidden among the trees and the sun rose high, then began to wheel over toward the west. Still there was no sign of the stagecoach.

'Maybe a horse broke down. Might've snapped an axle,' Dane Hoffman said as the two men sat side by side on a dry knoll.

'It's too early,' Faison believed. 'The passengers – if there are any – will be allowed to take a break

76

at Flyburg. Hell, you know all that, Dane!'

Yes, Hoffman knew all of that. He also knew from talking to old friends at the stage depot that today's coach was due to be carrying a large quantity of paper currency to the banks in Mesa. How much, no one knew exactly, but it was always a fair-sized amount, and the gold-dust from the claims on the upper Gila River had been flowing into town recently, filling the bank's coffers. The exchange was bound to be a large one. Hoffman knew that the one pay-day would make up for the years of work he would miss because of that damnable Calvin Poole.

If they could pull it off.

If that new man, the one they called Laredo, was not on board – but he would be, of course. One of the workers in the stage yard had mentioned hearing the man's name mentioned in Poole's office, and another laborer there had said:

'Laredo! If it's the man I'm thinking of, I know about him. He's got a long reputation, boys. If the banks brought him in, it's all over for the Chicolote Highwayman.'

Dane Hoffman rose and peered down towards the length of the desert road, seeing no dust rising. He knew that the stage was not very late. Mentally he was trying to find an excuse to call the whole thing off. He had made an agreement with

Stu Faison, but at heart he was no highwayman, only an unemployed stage driver with a grudge which, rather than growing stronger, seemed to weaken and wilt in the heat of the day. He should never have said he'd come along.

It must have been the whiskey.

Stu Faison, for his part, looked more determined than ever. But then the big man, a former shotgun rider, was a more daring type than Hoffman. Dane Hoffman turned back towards Faison, cuffing perspiration from his brow.

'Nothing.'

'It'll come,' Faison said with fading patience. Maybe, he thought, he should have left Dane back in Mesa and tried it alone. But two men had a better chance at it than one. Faison stood now himself and gazed out over the long desert. Heat veils shimmered on the white flats below. A single dark vulture drifted overhead. Faison saw a puff of dust, far away, and then it grew, becoming a long tail of sandy dust. He waited a minute longer to be sure; then, as if they could be overheard on that lonely mountain, said softly:

'It's coming, Dane. Let's find our positions.'

Dane Hoffman felt a trickle of cold horror run down his spine. He wanted no part of this, he realized with sudden certainty. But, with Faison's cold dark eyes on him, he reached for his blue silk bandanna, shifted it from front to back and tugged the mask up over his face.

# SIX

Hoffman and Faison hid behind trees on opposite sides of the trail. They could see the team of laboring horses, the driver's and shotgun rider's faces. Dane Hoffman glanced at the log they had rolled across the road and smiled beneath his mask. It just might work after all, *should* work.

The two men had made a series of miscalculations in their planning. For one thing, the shipment of new currency had been delayed for twenty-four hours. Secondly, the stage driver, Bert DeFord, was trying to get back on his feet after a year's lay-off following an injury and he was not about to lose his new job. Andy Patterson, riding shotgun, was experienced at his work, had seen most everything in his time, and he had the patience of a rogue bear.

And then, it was true that there were five passengers on board the Chicolote stage on this day, but all were rough and ready men heading for the Mesa River goldfield and they were in no mood to be robbed of the little they had.

So when Dane Hoffman stepped from behind the pine tree and stepped into the road, his rifle raised, and shouted in a rather shaky voice, 'Pull up that team and throw down your guns!' all hell broke loose.

Stu Faison had eased up along the side of the coach to try to get near enough to the shotgun rider to disarm him. He was within four steps of his goal when Andy Patterson bellowed out, 'Whip 'em, Bert!' and opened up with his shotgun, sending Dane Hoffman into a head-first dive towards safety. Faison tried to rush to the horses to grab their harness, but Bert DeFord had snapped his whip and the horses were already in motion.

Bert drove his team and following coach directly towards the log, there being no way round it. Stuart Faison yelled 'Stop!' fruitlessly, and his voice so near at hand caused men in the stage to peer out. All of them had guns in their hands and as the team of horses rumbled on, gunfire spewed from every window. Stu ran for the side of the road and flung himself into it, his mask falling from his face.

Bert was a determined driver now, and the log Hoffman and Faison had chosen proved to be a little too small. The horses cleared it and the stage jolted over, fracturing one spoke of a rear wheel, but doing little other apparent damage, and it rolled away through a thick cloud of dust, six men on board the stagecoach all firing back at the unlucky Hoffman and Faison.

Minutes later the coach had disappeared over the crest and started its downhill run. Faison and Hoffman sat defeated beside the road.

'That wasn't much as a piece of work, was it?' Dane Hoffman panted. Neither man had actually been hit during the wild shooting by the men riding the stage, but all of their shots had been far too close.

'It seems we need a little more practice,' Stu Faison said, letting his heavy shoulders rise and fall.

'You practice,' Dane Hoffman said, levering himself to his feet with the help of a nearby tree trunk. 'Me, if I can't get my driving job back, I'll try to find work mucking out a stable instead.'

Laredo rose in the morning, well rested, stretched his bare arms as he stood before the sunrise-tinted window of his hotel room, and slowly began to dress. He was still finishing with the snaps on his faded blue shirt when there was a tap on his door. He went that way and opened it to young Wilbur

Harrison, who looked a little pale and uneasy on this new morning. Harrison made his way to Laredo's mussed bed and seated himself, hat in hands.

'They're saying that we won't be having any outriders with us on this haul,' Harrison said.

Laredo finished tucking in his shirt. 'No, it takes time to authorize payment, to find the right sort of men for the job. These things can't be done overnight.'

'No, I suppose not.' Harrison watched Laredo strap on his gunbelt and recover his Stetson from a bedpost.

'It looks like you had an interesting night,' Laredo said. The young man's eyes were bleary. He seemed to tremble a little.

'In a way,' Wilbur said, his eyes shifting away from Laredo towards the red eastern sky which gleamed dully on the window pane of the hotel room.

'Want to tell me about it?'

'Ah . . . it was nothing, I don't suppose, Laredo,' Harrison said. He leaned back on his elbows. 'I went into this establishment down the street last night. A place called the Red Dog.'

'I've seen it,' Laredo replied.

'And what happens, but I meet this beautiful young woman named Goldie. She had the yellowest hair I ever did see – and man, Laredo, did she know how to dress fancy!'

'And so you sat down with her.'

'And so I did – why she would pick a man like me out of the crowd, I couldn't say. But we sat down and I had a few beers and Goldie ordered herself some drink like I've never seen. And she enjoyed talking to me! She told me so. She was hanging on every word I said. It was downright inspirational.'

'How long did you stay?' Laredo asked.

'Oh, I don't know. Time seemed to just fly past, you know. Goldie had an awful craving for those drinks she was ordering, and it was only gentlemanly to keep buying them for her. They didn't seem to affect her much at all,' Wilbur remembered.

'But sometime after midnight I had to be honest with Goldie and tell her that I couldn't buy her any more drinks because my money was running low, and I had to save up so that I would have some in the bank when I got around to asking Fortunata to many me. I guess I shouldn't have mentioned Fortunata, because although Goldie was still friendly, she wasn't so warm any longer, do you know what I mean?'

'I think so.'

'I guess I hurt her feelings which was not my

intention, but I couldn't afford to spend no more there. But,' he sighed, 'I suppose she got over it some, because when I left she was talking to some other men and smiling at them – though it wasn't the same as the way she had smiled at me. I had to tell her about Fortunata, didn't I, Laredo? I mean I felt bad, but. . . .'

'You did the right thing, Wilbur. Let's get down and have some breakfast, see that our stage is loaded and get the team hitched.'

'You're right,' Wilbur said, getting to his feet. 'Let's get back to work. I'll try not to think about the way I must've hurt Goldie's feelings.'

They started out an hour later, the new currency in a strongbox in the boot, the fresh horses moving eagerly. Wilbur Harrison shot one remorseful glance at the Red Dog saloon as they wheeled past it.

The young man's driving was much smoother on this morning; of course, the first stretch of the road was that long arrow-straight stretch across the alkali flats. In the distance across the white country the low hills sheltering the Fairmont cut-off waited, dark, squat and now vaguely menacing.

'Think we'll get through this time?' Wilbur shouted.

'We will,' Laredo said with a confidence he did

not feel. How could anyone know?

The sun rose higher, growing as white as the sandy desert itself. Alkali coated the backs of the horses and the clothing of the men. When the collection of ramshackle buildings that sheltered in the shade of the mountain slope appeared, Wilbur Harrison smiled.

It was the first time he had ever been happy to glimpse Flyburg. For there, at the last watering stop before the Fairmont, horses and men could rest, slake their thirst and even have a quick meal. To their left now, the dry, slate-sided Fairmont loomed tall, dark and challenging. There were no trees at all along its eastern flank, only yucca, nopal cactus and an occasional clump of red manzanita. It appeared as inhospitable as ever.

Wilbur slowed the team as they reached the outer edges of the 'town' of Flyburg: three low adobe buildings sweltering in the heat, and the wooden Chicolote Stage Line building with its attached barn and corrals.

'Eastbound coach is here!' Wilbur said, pointing towards the side of the line building where a team of impatient horses stood harnessed to another Chicolote stage.

'Poole must not be doing as badly as he claims,' Laredo answered, 'if he's got coaches running daily.'

'These boys will know what's happening up along the cut-off,' Wilbur said. 'They got through, at least.'

But perhaps the eastbound was carrying nothing more than a few passengers and a sack of mail. If there were spies inside Poole's organization, the highwayman – or *men* – wouldn't bother trying to stop it.

Inside the low wooden building which was separated into two sections with a freight office and depot on one side and a restaurant furnished with long plank tables on the other, they recognized the eastbound driver and his shotgun rider by their dress and the dust clinging to them, although neither Wilbur nor Laredo knew them by name.

'Let's have a talk with them,' Wilbur suggested.

'You do that. I'll be sticking close to that coach of ours and the load we're carrying. If you can get someone to make a sandwich up for me, I'd appreciate it, though.'

Laredo went out into the glare of the day and watched the station attendants watering the horses with their buckets. Unhitching all of the horses and leading them to water just took too long, and Calvin Poole wanted no time wasted when his coaches were running. Laredo leaned up against the shaded side of the stagecoach and listened to the constant humming of bees and wasps as they swarmed around the mesquite bushes near the stream and then darted off homeward. A cloud of gnats decided to investigate his head, and he waved the tenacious insects away.

When Wilbur Harrison reappeared he was excited. 'I brought you two sandwiches,' he said, handing over the small paper-wrapped bundle. He could hold it in no longer. He burst out with his news:

'They tried to stop the westbound stage yester-day. In the same spot.'

'They? More than one man?'

'They saw two highwaymen, but they fought their way past them. They had a log across the road again, but Bert DeFord whipped his horses over it. Broke a wheel, but no further damage.'

'Lucky for him. If a wheel had come off, he could have spilled the coach and injured everyone on board. Listen, Wilbur,' Laredo said as he unwrapped his sandwich, 'if that ever happens again, don't try doing what DeFord did. It's plain reckless.'

'All right,' Wilbur Harrison agreed, though he looked a little disappointed.

The stage continued its long course, making its slow way up the narrow steepening grade of the cut-off, the horses laboring, until they began to enter the dry pine forest once again and the road leveled out. Coming from this direction, the land fell away to their left while the timbered slopes rose to their right: the reverse of their earlier route. Still, it was easy enough to recognize the spot where the hold-ups had occurred. Wilbur again began to look uneasy, but Laredo briefly placed a hand on the young man's shoulder.

'They won't try it two days in a row. Not after what happened yesterday.'

'You sure of that, Laredo?'

No, Laredo wasn't sure. Because he was convinced now that the highwaymen were not a single group acting in concert. There could be two separate gangs or even three. It was perplexing, to say the least, but it probably didn't matter if he never got to the bottom of it, so long as the menace of the highwaymen was halted.

'There's the log,' Wilbur said, pointing at a length of pine that had been rolled aside, probably by the men aboard the eastbound stage.

'Why don't you pull up here for a minute,' Laredo said. 'I want to have a look around.'

Leaving an uneasy Wilbur Harrison in the box, Laredo swung to the dusty earth and walked a slow circle around the area. The wind was dry. A pennant of gauzy cloud stretched across the long sky. A squirrel chattered a warning at Laredo as he made his slow way through the trees. Once he crouched, studied something he had found. Then he rose again, dusting his hands on his jeans and returned to the stagecoach.

'Let's get going, Laredo. I won't be happy until we've reached Mesa again,' Wilbur said uneasily.

'Get them started then,' Laredo answered with a smile as he swung aboard, and Wilbur started the team with a sharp snap of his reins against their flanks. The forest thinned, the road began to tilt down. Mesa could not be seen in the distance yet, but it was ahead across open country. They were home free with the new currency for the three banks. That part of the job, at least, had been safely completed. But Laredo had not yet begun on his assignment.

Deacon Cody had given him his instructions: he wanted these highwaymen brought to justice as a lesson to others. That was going to prove to be a little trickier than bringing a strongbox of currency through safely.

And a lot more dangerous.

The tracks Laredo had found in the pine woods were a little confusing. Up until now he had assumed that the highwayman – or *men* – were making their escapes on the open desert in the general direction of a small town known as Tres Palmas. But the fresh imprints two horses had left at the hold-up site were heading back toward

Mesa. This seemed to confirm his conclusion that these stick-ups were being pulled off by disparate groups of men and not a single gang. It also confused the issue – Laredo obviously could not set out for Tres Palmas and make enquiries around Mesa town at the same time.

That these two riders were returning to Mesa seemed to indicate that they either lived there or had close contacts there. All right, he thought, as the stagecoach reached the long gray flats and Wilbur let the team line out towards home, he would assume that the two were from Mesa and he would tackle that side of the investigation first. After all, that was where he was bound himself.

'The only reason that the westbound stage got hit yesterday,' he said, thinking out loud now, 'was because the robbers assumed they would find bank money on board. They wouldn't have willingly stopped a coach carrying five hard, armed men had they had known.'

'I agree,' Wilbur said. He was feeling confident now, proud that he had completed his run, though he was no longer so sure that this was the way he wanted to make his living. He didn't wish to make Fortunata a widow. 'So what are you saying, Laredo?' he shouted above the clopping hoofs of the running team, the wind rushing past the swaying stage.

'It means that they had to have some inside information. Everyone, us included, thought that the currency would be on yesterday's stage. We ourselves didn't know until we got to Tucson that the shipment had been delayed for twenty-four hours. They had to have had inside information – only in this case it was mistaken information.'

'Not many people would be privy to the shipping schedule,' Wilbur shouted as the stage hit a shallow rut then straightened out again. 'Do you think one of the bankers talked at the wrong time?'

'Those bankers have lips so tight they can't whistle.'

'Then that only leaves ... someone from the Chicolote Stageline, doesn't it?'

'That's all it leaves,' Laredo agreed. 'Poole or someone close to him shot off his mouth and gave the information to the highwaymen, either intentionally, or more likely, accidentally.'

'Why "more likely"?'

'These robberies could be a disaster for Poole if they're not stopped – he is not going to give these thieves any help knowingly. It could have been some clerk in his office, I suppose, but the man would know that he would lose his job and likely go to prison if caught.'

'You know, those Chicolote men, almost all of

them that I've met so far, are loyal to Poole. Why would they tell some strangers about the shipment?'

'I'm not thinking of strangers,' Laredo replied, and for the time being he said no more. Now in the near distance they could make out the low cluster of dark forms appearing on the desert horizon. They were home.

Laredo watched the team being unharnessed, the smiling Wilbur Harrison receiving the congratulations of his new co-workers in the yard of Chicolote Stage Line. He himself stood guard at the boot of the coach. Several Chicolote employees had approached him to ask if he needed help in transferring the strongbox, but he refused them and instead sent a boy with a message and waited until Howard Tibbets and Joe Thrush appeared. The bankers had brought two armed, uniformed guards with them, and Laredo handed the currency over to them, accepted hastily expressed thanks and walked off uptown, feeling stiff and weary.

He first went to the stable to check on his buckskin horse, which eyed him over a stall partition as if it resented having being abandoned. He paid the stableman and saddled up.

Oddly, sore and spent as Laredo felt, there was something reviving about swinging aboard the buckskin and settling on to his familiar perch in the saddle. He wondered briefly if there was any point in checking in with Marshal Patrick Donovan, but thought not.

He already knew who the men he was after were.

# SEVEN

Laredo had given the matter long and serious thought on the way in to Mesa, and he believed he had come up with a solution to most of the mystery. The first highwayman had been identified as Hal Trevor, gunned down in his third attempt at a robbery. His motive had been revenge. The second man, they had no name for as yet. Frightened off, he had made his escape in the direction of Tres Palmas. The third was Mason Riddle, whom Calvin Poole, despite warnings, had hired to protect his interest. He had managed to make his escape with a lot of the banks' gold. When Laredo had shot Riddle, he had taken to the desert, in the direction of Tres Palmas. Tres Palmas would have to be looked at more closely.

For now that would have to wait. In an odd way there was a pattern to all of Calvin Poole's troubles. People didn't like him and he treated them like dirt. Hal Trevor, or so the story went, quit because Poole was making suggestive remarks about his young wife. Poole had fired a stagecoach driver and his shotgun rider just because they weren't equipped to halt a hold-up.

These two would hold a grudge for a long time. These two – Dane Hoffman and big Stu Faison – would know the workings of the stage line. It would be no trouble to them to find out which coach was supposed to be carrying gold for the east or currency to the west. Laredo wanted to talk to them. He hadn't asked at the stage depot because for all he knew they had a confederate still working there, a man who could convey inside information. He didn't want word getting out that he was hunting them.

Mesa wasn't that big a town and Hoffman and Faison were well-known there. The favorite hangout of the Chicolote employees was the Golden Eagle saloon. It was there that Laredo swung down from his buckskin as the sky began to purple in the west and the sheer clouds he had noticed earlier reddened in the dying sunlight. Men in twos or threes began to make their way towards the saloon as night settled, their work-days completed.

Laredo waited for one loud group to tramp up on to the boardwalk in front of the saloon and joined them as they proceeded inside; he was inconspicuous among them, or so he hoped. Even through the crowd of milling, shouting men he spotted them easily enough. They sat in a small round corner in the farthest end of the saloon as if trying to isolate themselves from everyone. The broad-shouldered Stu Faison was loosely clasping a half-empty mug of beer in both hands. Dane Hoffman had nothing in front of him. His eyes were turned down, his head hanging a little. Both looked trail-dusty and tired. Hoffman had a large bruise on one cheek. Laredo started that way, easing through the crowd of laughing, debating, bellowing men.

'Hello boys,' he said. As his shadow fell across, the table, Dane Hoffman lifted his eyes, defeat in their depths.

'You're Laredo?' he asked in a thin voice.

'That's right. I'd like you to come across the street with me and talk to the marshal.'

'Why would we want to do that?' Stu Faison asked truculently. His heavy shoulders shifted beneath his well-worn flannel shirt.

'Because it's the easiest way,' Laredo said. 'You're caught, boys.'

'No one saw us!' Dane Hoffman blurted out, then, realizing his mistake, he moaned softly. Maybe some of the men bound for the goldfields had stopped long enough to make a report to the marshal – and he did remember that one moment when Stu Faison's mask had slipped from his face. Had chance put someone aboard who knew Stuart? After all, he had worked for Chicolote for a time; maybe the driver had known him. He rubbed his eyes with one hand and nodded acquiescence.

'We'd better just give it up, Stu,' Hoffman said.

'Like hell I will!' Faison said and he rose suddenly, pushing the table aside so roughly that it nearly tipped. Then he flung himself at Laredo. The man was half as thick again through the chest as Laredo, and bull-mad. He lunged forward with both fists flying as Laredo backed away. Dane Hoffman slid his chair back against the wall, out of danger, and the crowd of drinking men surrounding them gathered in a circle to watch the fight.

Laredo kicked a chair in front of Faison, but it did little to slow him down. Faison backed Laredo against the bar and threw a powerful right hand shot that glanced off Laredo's temple. Laredo backed the man off with two hard jabs to his chin and then kicked him hard on the knee. Faison howled more in anger than in pain, bent forward and when he straightened up again, his eyes red and wild with fury, Laredo drove his forearm down against the bridge of Faison's nose. There was a sharp crack and for an instant Laredo thought he might have broken his own arm, but Faison's nose began spewing blood which immediately flowed down into his mouth and across his chin.

Faison, looking like a wounded grizzly, came forward again, meaty clenched fists held low.

The gunshot was near and deafening. Black powder-smoke filled the saloon; a chandelier rattled. The crowd parted to let Marshal Patrick Donovan pass among them and he halted three steps away from Laredo and Faison.

'What's this about?' Donovan asked as Laredo took one rapid step forward and disarmed Faison, slicking his Colt from his holster.

'Two of the highwaymen,' Laredo said. His skull was still ringing and he shook his head to try to silence the bells there. 'I think we'd better get them over to your office.'

'Two of them?' Donovan said in puzzlement, the muzzle of his revolver still fixed on Faison whose eyes had lost none of their belligerence. 'God's sake, Laredo, how many highwaymen are there!'

'That's what we have to talk about. Let's get these two over there,' Laredo said, nodding to include the defeated Dane Hoffman.

They walked out of the Golden Eagle that way – Hoffman in front, then Faison with the marshal's gun not far from his spine, then Laredo, who heard a few comments as he passed.

'That wasn't much of a fight.'

'I've seen better. Remember the night Willie Gordon tangled with. . . .'

Outside the starlit night was warm and still, quiet as they moved away from the noisy saloon. Inside the marshal's office Donovan asked Laredo, 'Want to talk to them first?'

'I think you'd better lock them up first,' Laredo replied, and Donovan nodded, taking a ring of heavy keys from a peg on the wall.

The marshal left the two behind bars, Hoffman sagged on a cot, his face in his hands, Stuart Faison clinging to the bars with a resentful scowl on his battered face.

Donovan replaced the key ring and sat down at his desk. He folded his hands and smiled faintly. 'I saw you going into the Golden Eagle, and from the look you had on your face, I knew there was a reason. Now, Laredo, suppose you tell me all about it.'

Laredo did, as concisely as possible, while Donovan sat there, a peaceful look on his face, nodding from time to time. Laredo concluded with, 'As for their part in it, I think Hoffman is ready to confess.'

'What you are telling me,' Donovan said, trying to clarify matters in his own mind, 'is that there was only one Chicolote highwayman and that after he – we know now that it was Hal Trevor – was killed, Mason Riddle and later Hoffman and Faison simply got the idea that it was a good way to get rich quick.'

'That about covers it,' Laredo agreed.

The marshal was doing some mental calculations. Now he counted on his fingers and lifted his eyes to Laredo. 'That leaves us still short one suspect.'

'I know it does. I think he's down in Tres Palmas, and I suspect that Mason Riddle fled there as well.'

'The two men are connected?'

'I don't know.' Laredo shrugged. 'Maybe if I can trace the two of them we'll find out.'

'You're going down there tonight?'

'I wouldn't ever find my way. It might even be difficult by full daylight.'

'I'd go with you, Laredo, maybe take a small posse along, but I've got my own town to watch.' Donovan said spreading his hands in apology.

'That's right, you have to think of your town first,' Laredo agreed, seeing the relief on Donovan's face as he told him that, 'It's your obligation; that's what they hired you for. Me, I was hired on to protect the banks' assets and to bring in men like these road agents.'

Donovan relaxed completely now, leaning back

in his chair to prop his boots up on his desk. As he did the front door burst open and the broad, excited and unwelcome Calvin Poole appeared. The stage-line owner tramped in, looking towards the cells, towards Laredo and then directly at the marshal as he crowded Donovan's desk.

'I hear you got them – there were some men talking in front of the Golden Eagle. Is that them?' he asked sourly, jabbing a thick finger towards the cell where Faison continued to glare threateningly and Dane Hoffman sat in abject despair.

'That's them.'

'I knew it. I told you that those two were no good, didn't I?' Poole looked gratified with his early solution of matters.

'Well, we don't think they had anything to do with the first hold-ups,' Donovan said slowly, showing little concern. Certainly he was not intimidated by Poole.

'Of course they did. Them and that devious Hal Trevor. They came up with a plan to wreck Chicolote Stage Line,' Calvin Poole said triumphantly. Laredo spoke now, coolly.

'No, Poole. That was your work.'

'What!' Poole turned in astonishment towards Laredo. 'Are you accusing me of plotting to rob my own stagecoach line?'

'No, sir,' Laredo replied calmly. 'I am telling you

that you almost single-handedly brought it to its knees by the way you do business, manage your men, make hasty decisions.' As Poole silently fumed, Laredo went on: 'It seems that Hal Trevor quit and then went on to wreak his revenge because you were annoying his wife. These two men,' Laredo said, indicating the two in the cell, 'decided to get even with you because you fired them, blaming them baselessly for allowing your stage to be held up.' Laredo lifted a silencing hand. 'Then there's the matter of you hiring Mason Riddle against all advice. Mason is a known thug, thief and killer. Why you thought he could be trusted is beyond me.

'No, sir, the way you handle men, the way you manage to put your own self-importance ahead of everything, even your own business interests, is the reason Chicolote Stage Company has come this close to failure.'

'Let me tell you—' Poole exploded, but Laredo didn't want to listen.

'Tell it to the marshal,' he said and walked out of the jailhouse. Just before he closed the door he had a last glimpse of Stu Faison in his cell, and there was an unexpected grin on the big man's face.

The town of Mesa was still up and rollicking, as much as a small town like that one could be said to rollick, but Laredo meant to be on the trail with the first light of dawn, so he returned to the hotel, ate a quick supper and climbed the stairs to his room, where weariness and a full stomach allowed him to drop off easily into a deep sleep.

The desert trail ended just five miles out of town. Leading nowhere, it just petered out and was swallowed by the trackless wasteland. Perhaps it had once been someone's intention to build a road leading somewhere in this desolate country, but who it was and what he might have had in mind were long ago erased by time and the desert sands.

Dawn had arrived with a flourish of color – deep violet, rose and burnt orange hues across the eastern horizon, but the heat of the rising sun had defeated these and the world went white again. There was no sign of the pearly clouds that had visited the area the day before. The sky was pale, empty and hot, as was the land across which Laredo traveled. The buckskin horse moved easily across the sand, but showed no liking for it.

In the scant shade of a lone creosote bush a jackrabbit sat panting. A desert kit fox, possibly stalking the hare, darted away as Laredo passed. Morning was white and long, and somewhere in the distance lay the pueblo of Tres Palmas where,

Laredo hoped, all of the mysteries of the Chicolote Highwaymen could finally be put to rest.

Ben Trevor sat on the patio of the cantina, staring morosely at his empty coffee cup. The thorny mesquite trees cast their familiar thin shadows across the heated ceramic Spanish tiles at his feet. A big man, the one they called Gordo, pushed his heavy cart laden with whatever he had managed to scavenge that morning and hoped to somehow resell, up the dusty street of Tres Palmas. A mockingbird landed among the thin branches of a mesquite, paused long enough to scold Ben Trevor, then fluttered away again on white-banded wings.

Whatever the bird had said, Ben figured that he deserved it.

He had had no luck in finding work. The truth was there was no work to be found in Tres Palmas for a man with few skills. Even skilled men were having difficulty finding jobs. Ben had been unable to find a way to help his dead brother's pregnant wife Margarita in her hour of need. It was enough to make a man, out of desperation, think again of attempting the reckless endeavor of robbing a stagecoach.

But Ben had failed miserably as a highwayman, and such thinking had caused his brother's death.

He folded his forearms on the table and rested his head on them. There had to be a way – isn't that what they told you? That there was always a way if you just looked hard enough? The big man with the scabbed, bristly face, his arm in a sling, emerged from the cantina and settled at the far table across the patio from Ben Trevor. He had brought a bottle of tequila and a glass with him.

Where had this one come from? Ben wondered.

Nobody came to Tres Palmas to see the sights, for the excitement, or even in search of business opportunities – none of these was to be found there. The big man was injured; perhaps he could not travel on until he was healed. What sort of injury? Ben found himself speculating. His horse could have thrown him of course. A hundred things could befall a man on the wide desert. Maria Corona would know – it was she who treated the wounded in Tres Palmas. Ben vowed to ask the medicine woman.

Why the wounded man stirred such curiosity in Ben Trevor he could not have said – or, yes, he could say. Whoever this man was he was not starved for ready cash. He ate well, he drank well, in the evenings he sometimes threw his money around, buying drinks for everyone.

He was the sort of visitor the poor town did not often see.

Perhaps, even if the stranger did not know it, he had plenty of money to spare.

It was dusk when Laredo dragged into Tres Palmas, the sky purpling, the shadows growing long and then fading into night. He walked his weary buckskin horse up the main street – the only street so far as he could see – looking for the facilities a traveling man expects, but he found nothing. There was nothing he saw resembling an inn or a public stable – there was little in the pueblo of Tres Palmas resembling anything at all. Crumbling adobes with their pole-frame ends poking out through the plaster, a scattering of half-naked kids and as many cur dogs, a closed *boutique*, and then at last, a cantina, which no town was without – could not long survive without.

Laredo guided his horse that way, wanting at least to find water and feed for his horse, a bed for himself.

He did wonder as he looped his reins around the hitch rail in front of the cantina why any of the highwaymen had chosen to return to a place such as this. Or perhaps he had it backwards: perhaps because they came from a place like this they felt they had no choice but to become highwaymen.

Laredo felt sympathy for all men, but in the end

it didn't matter so far as his job was concerned. Rich or poor, they were going to pay for their transgressions if he found them.

# EIGHT

When the warm evening had settled into the cool of night, Laredo found himself in a neat little room in a small house on the edge of town. Men in the cantina had been happy to show him a nearby farm where his horse could be fed and watered, and a woman on the farm had told him of a place where he could spend the night. The lady who owned the house, he had been told, was desperate for money and would welcome him.

Well, she had – after a fashion. The woman was young, slender, her glossy dark hair drawn back and held in place with a Spanish comb. She was also obviously full with child. Her name was Margarita. She studied Laredo hesitantly, touched her hair with nervous frequency. She was alone and had doubts about having a strange man in the house. The front door was left open even after

Laredo had been shown his room and had turned in.

'Sometimes,' Margarita had said, keeping her eyes turned down, 'my friends come over late. I have many friends. They're the sort who are welcome to walk in any time they feel like it.'

Smiling inwardly, Laredo pretended to accept her explanation. He knew she did not want him there, but the silver in his open hand had brightened her eyes. There was a small window high on the wall in the room where Laredo waited for sleep. Through it he could see a handful of silver stars. He yawned and tried to formulate a plan of action for morning. Outside of poking around and asking a few questions nothing came to mind. Coming all the way to Tres Palmas was probably a futile gesture. But he had told Cody that he would find the highwaymen – or had Cody told him that he would? Laredo smiled in the night, and after a little while he rolled over and went to sleep.

'Where did he come from?' Ben Trevor wanted to know, but Maria Corona could only shrug.

'He did not say.'

'But it was a bullet wound that you treated?'

'Do you want to see the bullet?' Maria asked. It was late; she was no longer young, and she wanted to go to sleep, but Ben Trevor had come pounding at her door, excitement in his eyes. Why this should be, she could not say. She did not understand men, had given up trying to many years ago.

'Where is he staying, Maria?'

'Ah, I don't know. I guess where I first saw him. He must still be there – in a back room at Esteban's.'

'Esteban Contreras?'

'Yes, Esteban Contreras,' Maria said, losing patience. She meant to make herself a small snack and then go to sleep. She only wanted this man to go away, much as she liked him, for Margarita's sake.

'I'm sorry to have bothered you,' Ben Trevor said, rising from the wooden chair he had been seated on. Maria's impatience was obvious. She waved a dismissive hand. *Just go!* She seemed to be saying with the gesture. Ben did so.

Outside the night was warm, the skies clear, the town silent except for the muted sounds of men's voices from the cantina. Ben started along the alleyway. A silent, eagerly sniffing white dog followed him for a way before he shooed it off. Somewhere a flock of chickens complained loudly and flapped their wings. Perhaps something had gotten into the henhouse. No lights burned across town. All of the windows were dark, the people of

111

Tres Palmas performing their private rites behind them.

Ben circled the block and crossed the main street, striding towards the sandy alley behind the cantina. There another dog lay, this one with its lip curled showing white fangs. Ben kicked at it, missed, and the dog scuttled away, tail between its legs. Behind the cantina was an open door. Empty boxes, a broken barrel and a pile of bottles lay in disorder. He crept towards the door, peering in cautiously.

Men were gathered at the long bar. Someone said something he couldn't hear and another man laughed. Across the room, in the farthest corner, sat the man with the wounded arm. He was still there then! Good. Ben withdrew silently and made his rapid way towards the house of Esteban Contreras. He had at least a little time, for he had noticed Contreras drinking in the cantina as well. He was temporarily wealthy with the largesse of his house guest. The stupid dog emerged again and tried to nip at his pantleg as he darted past. Ben kicked savagely at it, found that he was perspiring, that his chest felt tight. He hurried on.

The front door to the small adobe house was open. Doors in Tres Palmas were never barred unless someone was trying to sleep or make love – what did they have to protect from thieves? Ben eased inside cautiously nonetheless. The ceiling was low, the room holding the heat of the day. As his eyes adjusted he could make out the outlines of rough furniture – a table, four chairs, a cupboard.

He crossed the room and entered a short hallway leading to two facing bedroom doors. Cautiously he advanced that way. The door to his right swung open easily at his push. It was Esteban's room, had to be. The clutter of a lifetime filled the dresser, spilled out across the floor.

The door to the left, however, opened on a nearly empty room. Low wooden bed, one chair, a leaning dresser with three drawers. Glancing towards the front door, Ben Trevor quickly entered, quickly crossed the room and struggled to open the top drawer of the dresser which had come off its rails.

There was little there. A jar of salve, a razor, a bar of yellow lye soap.

And a bandanna.

Ben Trevor frowned. The scarf was of dark-blue silk, and it was nearly identical to the one he had worn on that one misguided day – and exactly the same as the one Hal Trevor had used to mask his face as the Chicolote Highwayman. It could not be coincidence. Ben fingered the bandanna and unfolded it cautiously. Wrapped inside the scarf was a small glass bottle, about twice the width of a man's finger and about as long. It had a cork in its mouth, but the vial was empty.

Ben picked the small bottle up. There was not enough light seeping into the room to see by, and so he struck a match although he already knew what he had found. By the sudden flare of the flame he could see tiny specks of mineral shining as only one metal does.

The vials, he knew, were what the banks used to ship measured gold dust. They were normally packed together in wooden containers, ten to each small box to make them easier to count. Frantically then, Ben Trevor began searching the room, knowing that at any time the front door might open and Esteban or the man with the wounded arm, or both, would return to find him there.

Half an hour's desperate search revealed nothing. Wherever the rest of the gold was, it was not here. Ben knew that he could waste no more time. He arranged things as he had found them, briefly regretted having struck a match since the telltale scent might linger, and with his heart hammering and his mouth dry, he plunged out of the house into the open air of the night.

He walked on as rapidly as he could for two dusty blocks. Eventually he sat down behind the closed store, using an upturned crate for a seat. He watched the alley as guiltily as any escaping thief does, but of course no one was following him.

Slowly, as the stars glimmered overhead in the blue-black sky and no sound could be heard across the lonesome desert town, he felt himself recover his native coolness, and he thought deeply about what he must do. The stranger, the man with the wounded arm was one of them – one of the highwaymen. Except that unlike Ben Trevor, this man had made his escape with a strongbox filled with gold. It seemed that he had paid a price for that gold, but nevertheless he had it.

Whereas Ben had nothing. Margarita had nothing. Ben had always admired his brother's strong principles in returning what he had only stolen to agitate Calvin Poole, but now Ben had nothing at all. Margarita and her unborn baby had profited nothing from Hal Trevor's escapades. Yet this man with the broken arm obviously had.

Was taking the stolen gold from him – if it could be found – the same as common thievery? Perhaps, Ben thought, he could take a portion of the gold and return the rest to the Chicolote Company, telling them that that was all he could find. That the man with the broken arm must have spent the rest. The idea seemed sound, and Ben was not impeded by moral considerations at this point. It had come down to survival.

He meant to discover where the man with the wounded arm had hidden the rest of the gold. And he meant to have his share of it.

Wilbur Harrison was walking tall on this sunny morning. He had been summoned to Calvin Poole's office where he expected to be congratulated for his work. Just the night before, his confidence soaring he had proposed to his Fortunata. Then the two – this shy girl and her spindly suitor – had gone hand in hand to tell her parents. Her father, gruff, silver-haired, wearing a drooping mustache had scowled and said little. If this skinny youth was the one she had chosen, though, he would not stand in her way. So long as the young rascal could support her.

'There's no worry there,' Wilbur told Fortunata's father in a bolder voice than he would have dared only a few days before. 'As you may have heard, I'm now a driver for the Chicolote Stage Line. It's steady work, steady pay.'

In truth Wilbur did feel secure. He was now learning the road with all of its twists and turns, growing familiar with his regular team of horses and their quirks. He and Laredo had brought through the last shipment of currency for the town's banks without a hitch, and the highwaymen were all in jail or had been driven off.

Fortunata had even let him kiss her in the pale moonlight.

He rapped confidently on the outer door to Calvin Poole's office and was admitted by Hyde, Poole's pale-eyed secretary, who ducked into the inner sanctum and returned. 'You can go in,' Hyde said with a nod of his head.

Inside the large, low-ceilinged office Calvin Poole, coatless, sat behind a massive if otherwise unremarkable desk. He glanced up at Wilbur as if annoyed.

'Good morning, Mr Poole,' Wilbur said, his hands turning his hat which he had removed on entry to the sanctum.

' 'Morning, Harrison. I just need a word with you. It won't take long.' Poole's expression changed only slightly. His eyes shifted briefly away. 'We're going to have to let you go.'

Wilbur was stunned. He could find no words. The room seemed to cant under his feet.

'But, sir . . .' he eventually managed to stutter. 'Hasn't my work been adequate?'

'Adequate?' Calvin Poole tasted the word for a moment or two. 'Yes, it has been so far, Harrison. But you were hired on temporarily, were you not? And now Bert DeFord has come back to work. He is a much more experienced man – why, the way he brought those passengers through the other day was remarkable. He's had years on the line, Harrison, you can't expect me to let him go and have an inexperienced man replace him.'

'No, sir, but—'

'There just isn't room for you, Harrison. I can't afford to carry extra drivers on the payroll. I'm sorry, but—'

'I'll work in the yard. Anything that—'

'Sorry. I have all the yardmen I need as well. Each of them with years of experience.' Poole started to rise, did not. 'That's just the way it has to be. Check in from time to time. If anything comes up, you'll be the first man we call. Have Hyde find out what's due you, and collect your pay.'

There was nothing else to say. Desolately Wilbur accepted the few dollars owing and went out again into the morning which seemed no longer bright and full of promise, but oppressively hot, dusty, empty and long as the desert beyond the town.

What was he to tell Fortunata? With his shoulders bowed, Wilbur walked the length of the street aimlessly, going nowhere. Where was there to go? In front of Tabor's General Store he sat down on a wooden bench and scowled at the stingy town. An old man sprouting white whiskers sat down at the other end of the bench, stoked and lit a pipe and stared out at the same bleak landscape. Wilbur found the man's presence depressing somehow.

He rose and strode away.

He was gazing towards the desert, beyond it, towards the Fairmont Range and he stopped dead in his tracks, standing in the middle of the dusty street as it came to him.

There was a way out of this.

If a man had the nerve – and was desperate enough. Just then Wilbur Harrison was that desperate. It was too early to visit Fortunata; she was not allowed to have visitors before noon. It was not too early to cross to the emporium and purchase the blue silk bandanna he would need.

'Who is that?' Mason Riddle asked in a low voice as the bartender at the cantina in Tres Palmas placed a bottle of yellow tequila on the table before Riddle. He lifted his chin toward the tall stranger leading a buckskin horse down the rutted main street.

'Him? I don't know,' the barman said, wiping his hands on his stained white apron.

He looks familiar, Riddle thought and he probed his memory, almost found the elusive information he was searching for, and then lost it again.

'I don't know,' the barman said, holding out his hand.

'Of course you don't,' Riddle growled, slipping

a few silver dollars from his vest pocket with his good hand. 'Nobody in this town knows anything.'

'That is true,' the bartender answered with a suave smile. He closed his hand around the silver coins and walked away across the tiled patio. Mason Riddle continued to watch the stranger with the buckskin horse, scowling. When the tall man was out of sight, Riddle poured a healthy dose of tequila into his glass and continued his brooding.

Riddle was running low on cash money. Of course he had resources hidden away, but to recover them he would have to make a long ride out on to the desert, and his arm still plagued him. If only that bastard hadn't shot him. . . . He sat up sharply.

He knew who the stranger was! Recognition flooded into his mind. That was the stage guard who had plugged him up along the Fairmont. That was exactly who he was! Had he come hunting Mason Riddle? The idea seemed far-fetched. Why would the stage company send a man out to hunt him down? But the coincidence was too great to ignore.

Riddle poured himself another drink, but this time he swallowed it nervously. Everything could be lost if this man was hunting him, if he found him. There seemed to be little choice suddenly. He could run. . . .

Or he could kill the tall man before he had the chance to kill Riddle. . . .

The tequila bottle and one of its brothers rode in Mason Riddle's saddle-bags as he started out of Tres Palmas on to the long white desert. In the end Riddle had decided to make a run for it. There was no profit in gunning down a man in a strange town where they might decide to hang him for the citizens' amusement. The tall man had not seen him yet, or if he had, he had given no indication of it. There was gold ahead of Riddle and only the possibility of death behind him. Much as he thirsted for revenge, he knew that now was not the time and Tres Palmas was not the place to take it. Now, if the tall man were bold enough to try following Riddle out on to the desert, that became a different story entirely. The desert sands concealed thousands of unmarked graves.

Riddle's arm throbbed and burned, the jolting stride of his horse did nothing to help matters. It was a beautiful animal but ungainly. He had regained some movement in that arm and had discarded his encumbering sling. It hurt, it would continue to hurt, but recovering the gold dust that he had hidden away would go a long way towards softening the pain.

Riddle glanced behind him, watching for anyone who might be following, but there was no one, nothing but endless desert. He reached back clumsily to his saddle-bags and removed the half-empty bottle of tequila riding there. Swallowing the raw liquor, he thought:

Things had gone badly, but from here on they could only improve.

Ben Trevor stood motionless in the shade of the overhanging stable roof. He watched the lone rider straddle that distinctive white horse with the gray mane and tail, noted his direction and then turned away, excitement growing. So, Riddle was making his run at last. Where else would he be going, but to collect the hidden gold, and Ben Trevor was suddenly sure of where the outlaw had hidden it.

He rushed back towards Margarita's house to collect saddle, canteens and extra ammunition that he figured to be needing. He wanted to tell her that her days of trouble were nearly behind her, but did not dare. He wanted to retain her respect. Most of all he wanted to take care of her and her newly arriving child. His brother's child.

There was one other reason for his surge of excitement. It was something that dwelt deep, lived in his very blood. Calvin Poole, it was said in Mesa, was the man who had gunned down Hal Trevor. That made Ben's obligation take root much deeper than did any other consideration.

It was a matter of honor that he kill Mason Riddle.

He hurried to the house, found the door standing open and rushed inside to find himself face to face with Laredo. 'I just came for my saddle. . . .' Ben began. Then he was silent.

Margarita turned away from the mirror on the wall. She had fixed her hair, pinning it up off her ears, ears where the stolen diamond earrings shone. She wore a certain flush of proud womanhood about her that could not be explained but seemed to be intertwined with her pregnancy. Her rounded belly enhanced her beauty rather than diminishing it. Her brown eyes were shining nearly as brightly as the diamonds in the stolen jewelry. Her lips were supple. Slightly parted in an unspoken question. Ben loved her more at that moment than he ever had; she was as close to angelic as any living woman can come.

The presence of the tall man jolted him out of his reverie. He became sharply aware of Laredo's searching eyes, the set of his jaw. His hand was draped casually over the butt of his holstered Colt revolver.

Ben shook his head and clenched his fists. At last he said to Laredo, 'My name's Ben Trevor, I guess you're looking for me.'

# NINE

Laredo stood frowning at the young man who had burst into the house where he had gone to collect his few belongings and pay Margarita. Unexpectedly outgoing on this day, perhaps because the sun was shining brightly and she now had no need to fear the traveling stranger, she had run to her room and returned, displaying the diamond earrings proudly.

'My husband gave them to me,' Margarita said. 'They are the last present he ever brought me.'

Laredo had not replied, only waited while she attached them to her earlobes and turned so that he could watch them shine and glitter in the morning light.

'Are they not beautiful. . . ?'

That was when Ben Trevor had rushed into the house, breathless and agitated. Seeing Laredo he had come to a dead stop then, gaping at both Margarita and the tall man. Blurting out his question to Laredo, Ben had stood quivering, expecting the worst. Laredo glanced at Margarita, noticing her failing smile and then replied:

'No, I'm not looking for you. Why would I be?'

'I just thought . . . it doesn't matter,' Ben mumbled.

Laredo shrugged a farewell and walked past Ben Trevor into the harsh morning sunlight. He had a good idea what that was all about, but there was no point in pursuing it just then. Instead he walked to the farm, picked up his buckskin, paid the farmer who had been watching him and rode a half a mile out of town where he swung down in the shade of a large old cottonwood.

He waited as the day grew warmer and the insects swarmed around him.

Half an hour on he saw Ben Trevor riding his way on a little sorrel with a white diamond on its nose. Trevor had blurted out that he wanted his saddle, and so plainly he had intended to ride out. Where? Ben Trevor clearly had some involvement in matters; how much Laredo could not be sure, but he wished to find out.

Laredo let the man pass by and then slowly followed after him.

They crossed white desert. The buckskin was

126

hock-deep in sand, deeper at times. This was the reason the Fairmont cut-off had been constructed in the first place. Coach and horses had a difficult time negotiating the terrain out on the flats. The cut-off, though steep, boasted hard underlying soil.

Laredo lifted his eyes, squinting into the sunlight. Ahead now he could see a rising red sandstone bluff. It lay low and long across the horizon. Secretive, anomalous, Laredo thought he knew what it was. He had heard men talking about the Honeycomb. As he drew nearer he could see that the bluff was indeed riddled with caves, hundreds, perhaps thousands of them. It was here they said that Hal Trevor, the first Chicolote Highwayman used to leave his stolen goods to be recovered by Poole, usually with a short sardonic or taunting note to the stage line owner.

He came upon a dry wash with a gravel bottom, gray willow brush lining its course. Laredo guided the buckskin that way, both to save the horse the labor of the sands and to take advantage of its concealment. The wash was twenty feet deep, shadowed, but the heat was as oppressive as it was on the flats. Sweat trickled into his eyes and stained his shirt front. His passing stirred a young cottontail rabbit into motion. It wove its way through the dry willow brush without making a sound in its passing. A covey of desert quail scattered before him. Apart from these there seemed to be nothing living in the canyon.

Laredo was mistaken. He cursed himself silently for his inattention, because a voice, soft and menacing, vaguely familiar called to him from out of the dense brush.

'Why don't you just turn that horse around and go back in the direction you came from?'

'Trevor?' Laredo said and there was a long pause before the man answered.

'Never mind who it is. I told you what to do.'

'You won't shoot me,' Laredo said.

'Why not? No one would ever know, not out here.'

'You're going to have to talk to me, tell me what this is all about.'

'I don't have to do anything!' Ben Trevor shouted hoarsely. 'Just get out of here – I'm going to lose him if I don't get back on his trail.'

'Lose who?' Laredo's voice was cool. It shouldn't have been, not with a concealed man's gunsights fixed on him, but Laredo had learned to control his words; sometimes a calming response could disarm a man who was apparently bent on violence. It was that or go to shooting.

Laredo watched the tangled brush closely, watching for movement, a bit of color, sunlight on metal, because if he was forced to, he would open up at any offered target. Maybe Ben Trevor sensed that. The man was no killer anyway. There was a defeated quality to Trevor's voice when he spoke again.

'It's the big man – the one who was carrying his arm in a sling.'

'Mason Riddle?' Laredo asked. He was only a little surprised.

'Yes. Him,' Ben Trevor answered. 'I just know he has a stash of gold-dust hidden up here.'

In a way that figured. Riddle had tried to disguise himself as Hal Trevor, had stopped the coach in the same exact spot the dead highwayman had preferred. Riddle was willing to take clues from what had been successful. Why would he not utilize the Honeycomb as a place to hide his loot as Hal had? Except Mason Riddle would be sending no note to the marshal's office to tell them where to recover the stolen goods.

'You'd better let me help you in this,' Laredo said, trying to calm the concealed rifleman.

'Why would I trust you!'

'Why would you not?' Laredo asked in the same even voice.

'You know why I'm following Riddle.'

'I have a suspicion,' Laredo said. 'Have you considered that the banks might give you a fair reward for returning the gold dust?'

Ben was silent, considering that. 'How would I know that's what would happen?'

'I guess you don't. But you don't really want to go on the outlaw trail, running and hiding for the rest of your life, do you?'

'No . . . no, I don't. Your solution is better than mine, I suppose,' Ben Trevor said, and with a rustling of brush, he appeared on the trail, his rifle now held loosely. 'It's just that I have been a little desperate lately,' he admitted to Laredo.

'Because of the woman?'

'Yes, because of Margarita! You've met her. She doesn't deserve to have to try raising an infant in poverty.'

'Nor does it help her if you're killed trying some mad scheme,' Laredo said and now his voice had chilled a little. There was a time for cajoling, a time for bullying.

'I thought you wanted to arrest me,' Ben Trevor said. 'It all began with the diamond earrings.'

'Did you steal them?'

'I did not, but. . . .'

'Even if you had I wouldn't take a hand. I work for the Territorial Bank Examiner – in the enforcement arm – I don't arrest men for stealing a horse, kicking a dog, getting drunk or punching a neighbor in the face. I couldn't if I wanted to. My authority is limited to protecting the banks' assets and capturing those responsible. Who those diamond earrings belong to, I couldn't care. If Marshal Donovan wants to investigate some day, that's his business.'

Ben Trevor smiled faintly and lifted a hand in a shrugging gesture. Both men knew that it would take a lot more than a pair of missing earrings to prod Patrick Donovan out of his office chair – and the matter was not even his bailiwick's responsibility.

'Let's get after Riddle before we lose him,' Laredo said.

The gully opened up after another quarter of a mile, fanning out on to the desert. They were nearly in the shadow of the Honeycomb. The red bluff loomed ahead, bleak and primitive-looking.

'Indians used to live in some of the larger caves,' Ben Trevor said as they rode side by side toward the monolith. 'Outlaws, lost travelers and a few crazy desert rats opposed to civilization in all its forms. A lot of the caves are interconnected. It's a regular maze inside. They say men who tried too explore it too deeply have been lost in the Honeycomb and never found their way. I don't think anyone's been around for years now, though. The creek's run dry, as you saw, and there's no way anyone could survive long here.'

Laredo saw the mouths of several large caves yawning wide, dozens – hundreds? – of smaller caves faced the desert as if the blast from some huge weapon had peppered them into the red sandstone. It was a desolate and disquieting place. They had not tried to cut Riddle's sign, for the white sand kept only imperfect tracks which did not long remain. And they had not wished to expose themselves unless it was necessary. Riddle was a conscienceless killer, and they had to assume that he had the high ground.

They paused beside a small broken stack of layered red stone and studied the bluff before them.

'I don't see his horse,' Ben said in agitation, wiping the trickling perspiration from his brow. 'Maybe he's already come and gone.' He resented Laredo for having made him stop and talk when he could have been hot on Mason Riddle's trail.

'If he has, then we'll have to follow him, but I think he's still around somewhere close.'

Laredo had no real reason for believing that other than his experience and a certain sense he possessed when trailing a man. Riddle would prob-ably be in need of rest, especially since he was still injured. He would figure that he had the time to load the gold on to his horse and carefully survey his backtrail before making his run.

'Then what are we waiting for?' Ben Trevor asked impatiently.

'Why give him the first shot?' Laredo answered. 'As it stands now, we don't know where he is holed up, but he can sure see us if we just ride out in the open.'

Trevor grumbled a response and sagged to his haunches, using the shade of the rockpile. It did little in the way of offering coolness, but it seemed better than the sun-white desert. Both men waited, sweat trickling down their chests, from under their arms, dribbling down their spines.

A horse whickered in a nearby cave and Ben leapt to his feet. Both pairs of eyes searched the Honeycomb for movement.

'Could you tell where it came from?' Ben Trevor asked in a gravelly whisper.

'Not for sure – we know it has to have been from one of the larger caves, though. The horse didn't crawl inside.'

'I think it must have been the one to the left,' Ben said. There were only two caves large enough to admit a horse yet near enough for them to hear the animal. Similar in appearance, with roughly arched entrances, it was difficult to choose between them. If there was a way of making their way on to the flats without being seen they could find the horse's tracks easily enough but there was no way. If Mason Riddle was watching, he would cut a man down before he had gone fifty feet.

Yet, Loredo considered, the man must be busy just then, trying to hoist the strongbox and tie it on his horse with the use of only one good arm. He figured they had to take the chance.

'Let's ease over to our left, then work our way back along the base of the bluff. In that close he won't be able to see us – or at least, he'll have no good rifle shot shooting down at that angle.'

Ben looked doubtful, but he was even more determined than Laredo. His own idea had been to simply ride their horses at a dead run toward the bluff and swing down before Riddle was aware of their approach. Laredo's plan, he admitted, was better. The more silently they approached, the better. He nodded his head and they moved on foot away from the caves, running in a crouch, boots silent against the heavy sand.

The sand made for tough going but they managed to reach the bluff without drawing a shot from above. They stood panting in the shadow cast by the red cliff. Laredo was drenched in sweat. He wiped his hands on his jeans and told Ben:

'There's the two caves. Which one do you want?'

'We're going to separate?'

'It's best, I think.'

'Well then, I still think the sound came from the

nearer one. I'll work my way toward it.'

'All right,' Laredo said. 'Let me go first. I'll take a position near the far cave, just in case you were wrong. If I hear shooting, I'll come on the run.'

Ben could only nod. His lungs were dry, his nerve unraveling. He was not cut out for this sort of work. He watched as Laredo moved off keeping close in to the bluff. He rounded a corner of the landform and was gone. Ben Trevor took in a deep breath and started on his way toward the near cave, wishing that Laredo had stuck beside him. This was trouble, real trouble and he knew it. The only thing that kept Ben plodding on was his determination to do something, anything to help Margarita. He could not run now.

Laredo edged his way along the bluff only glancing up as he passed the cave where Ben thought he had heard the horse whicker. He could not see the mouth of the cave, could see no easy way up over the jumble of red rock, and studying the sandy flat he could see no trace of a horse's passing. That was not surprising. A horse's hoof made indefinite prints in such material, and these soon caved in or were covered by the gusting desert wind. The day grew no cooler. The sun was at its zenith and seemed determined to remain there. Laredo went on, eyes and ears alert for any movement, any small sound. There was no doubt that Mason Riddle would fight. He was not the sort to surrender.

The second cave that Laredo came to seemed more promising to his eyes. There was a sort of ramp of broken red stones that a horse could be led up. Again, he saw no signs of an animal having passed over the sandy earth beyond, but the first cave had seemed to offer no access. If Riddle was up there, it had to be in this cave.

Laredo placed his rifle aside, figuring the long gun would be of little use in the close confines of a cave, drew his Colt and began to ease his way up along the stony ramp. Riddle was there. He was suddenly sure of it; every sense in his body tingled. It was a primitive emotion that many modern men doubted, but Laredo had spent most of his adult years hunting, and he paid much attention to his sixth sense when it spoke. Now it was speaking. Riddle was up there.

Laredo was forced to go to all fours to inch his way upward. The last few feet were agonizing. With his Colt clenched in his right hand, it was difficult to ascend; his boot toes had to fumble for purchase, since Laredo refused to allow himself to glance back to see where they were placed. His eyes had to be kept on the mouth of the cave. A stone rolled from under his boot and bounced down the slope, its noise intolerably loud in the stillness of the desert day. If Riddle heard that. . . .

The highwayman could simply lean out, look and blow Laredo's head off.

But no one appeared in the shadowed cave mouth. A small sound from within caught Laredo's ear. Metal clinking against stone. The horse had shifted its feet, perhaps finding it uncomfortable to be laden with an iron strongbox. Laredo figured he had nothing to gain by waiting longer. It could be that Mason Riddle was busy with his task. It might be that he had heard Laredo making his approach and was waiting only for him to show himself. Laredo incongruously thought then of Deacon Cody, and reflected for a fraction of a second that this was why they paid him; this was where his money was well-earned.

Laredo gathered himself and rushed up across the rugged stones and into the cavern.

# TEN

After the sun-bright day outside, the cave was a pit of darkness. Laredo entered it by rolling to one side ready to answer any gunfire he might provoke. He lay nearly under the belly of a white horse with a gray mane and tail. The horse shied nervously away, not liking the rude intrusion. The clop of its steel-shod hoofs echoed deeply through the cave.

Riddle was not here.

If he was, he had not fired. Why? Laredo got slowly to his feet, his eyes probing the dark recesses of the cave, the muzzle of his pistol searching this way and that. The cavern was deeper than Laredo had expected. He could not tell how far back into the bluff it ran, but surely fifty feet or more.

And the horse was not yet burdened with the stolen gold.

Laredo eased past the animal, running a soothing hand along its body from flank to neck. Was Riddle only now retrieving the stolen gold-dust from some inner vault? That had to be it. Wait for his return then, or. . . .

The boom of four shots sounded in the close confines of the cave. The white horse danced away and Laredo ducked into the interior compartment of the cavern. A voice, full-throated and deep yelled:

'Where in hell did you come from!'

That was Riddle. It meant that somehow Ben Trevor had managed to find a passageway between the two caves in the Honeycomb, and surprised Mason Riddle at his work. It also probably meant that Trevor was now dead.

Laredo eased down the passageway, keeping his back to the wall, his pistol held, barrel up, beside his ear. There was a shuffling sound ahead, a grating noise. Mason Riddle appeared dragging the strongbox along with his wounded arm. His pantleg showed signs of a recent bullet wound. His thigh was bleeding deeply.

Laredo stepped out, gun leveled.

'You might as well give it up, Riddle. There's no way out.'

Riddle emitted a pained, growling sound like that of a wounded, desperate animal – which he was – and dropped the strongbox to draw his pistol. He fired wildly in the darkness, and the flame from the muzzle briefly blinded Laredo. He went to one knee as the bullet pinged off the stone of the shaft and whined off into the distance. Riddle brought his pistol up for a second try, but he never triggered that one off.

Laredo was first, and his Colt sent a deadly .44 slug across the narrow distance between them. The heavy lead bullet slammed into the big man's chest, driving him back. As Laredo watched Riddle dropped to both knees, glared up at him and pitched forward on to his face, his handgun clattering free against the stone floor of the cave.

Laredo crouched over Riddle, but the big man was beyond help. A thin, injured voice called from deeper in the shaft:

'Help me. I need help.'

Laredo walked on, eventually finding a dark, low-ceilinged nook where Ben Trevor sat limply propped up against the wall of the cave. Blood was staining the front of his white shirt heavily. He lifted his eyes to meet Laredo's concerned gaze.

'He wasn't half as good as I thought he was,' Ben

said unsteadily. 'He fired three times, only hit me once.'

It seemed to Laredo that once might have been enough. Trevor was hit high on the chest. It was difficult to tell how much damage the bullet had done, but the wound was bleeding copiously. At least the bullet had not hit a lung, for there was no froth in the blood.

'Did I get him?' Ben Trevor asked.

'In the leg. How'd you get here?'

'I clambered up into the other cave,' Ben said, breathing raggedly as Laredo removed and tore Trevor's shirt up for bandages. 'There was no one there. I poked around and found a passageway and followed it along. I emerged here just in time to see Riddle towing the strongbox off. He turned and – well, you see what happened.'

'Come on, let's get you out of here,' Laredo said, crouching to allow Ben Trevor to throw an arm over his shoulders. Together they limped toward the entrance to the cave. Laredo could feel the seep of Trevor's hot blood on his own arm.

'What about the gold?' Ben Trevor asked.

'I'll come back for it.'

'It's time we split up,' Ben said in a strangled voice.

'I'll get you home.'

'No, I mean it!' Trevor said with some vehemence. 'I can make it back to Tres Palmas – I have to. Maria Corona can patch me up. She's good with gunshot wounds. You, Laredo, you can't leave that gold here. Not just for the banks' sake, but for mine.' He gripped Laredo's shirt front strongly with one hand. 'What if you go off and leave it and someone else stumbles across it. What would happen to Margarita then? If you can get the dust back to Mesa . . . maybe get a reward for me, like you said . . . then whether I make it or not, she'll have something, Laredo. Don't you see?'

'I see,' Laredo agreed reluctantly. 'All right, then. If that's the way you want it. Let's get you down to your horse, Ben.'

It was difficult but they got Ben Trevor mounted and on his way to Tres Palmas. Laredo watched as the man, limp in the saddle, bent forward across the withers of his pony, made his slow, painful way southward. He could only wish him well.

Laredo returned to the cave and continued his work.

With two horses now and two sets of saddle-bags, Laredo was able to leave the strongbox behind, and load the gold dust, dividing it evenly between his buckskin and Mason Riddle's beautiful white horse. The sun was still high when he rode back on to the desert, leading Riddle's pony. He did nothing with the outlaw's body, leaving it to the ghosts of the Honeycomb.

It was late afternoon when Laredo, having bypassed Flyburg, reached the Fairmont cut-off. The horses both seemed pleased to find the firm purchase of the Fairmont underfoot, and although the road was steep, especially on this side of the grade, the going was easier than across the soft sand desert. Also, the land was in shadow now that the hot sun was floating toward the far horizon and the afternoon grew cooler, even though the bulking mass of the Fairmont shielded them from the western breeze.

The rocky slope on this side, the Flyburg side, grew nothing but tall flowering yucca, immense patches of nopal cactus and manzanita. Lately prized for its glossy red bark, manzanita wood had become fashionable for the making of sturdy if twisted walking-sticks.

Laredo and his now-tiring horses crested the grade an hour or so before sunset. The yellow sun sprayed harshly against the sky which was now cooling to pale blue. The pine trees along the ridgeline, dry and dusty as ever, nevertheless offered cooling shade. The breeze was fresher atop the mountain, and Laredo felt like a man revived.

143

If Poole was keeping to the old schedule, there should be an eastbound stage coming before long, carrying yet more gold dust from the Upper Gila strike. They would have news from Gila. Laredo found himself wondering about the fate of Dane Hoffman and Stu Faison – certainly they had been guilty of attempting a hold-up, but perhaps there was at least the slimmest chance that Calvin Poole would show some mercy in prosecuting them. Men who cannot find work may be driven to extremes.

There are many things that can drive men to extremes, Laredo reflected, and that was the history of the Chicolote Highwaymen: Hal Trevor, incensed at Poole's attempted seduction of his wife, Margarita, his brother, Ben, wanting to provide for his brother's widow – for Laredo no longer entertained doubts about who the second highwayman had been, and Dane Hoffman and Stu Faison, both fired because they had not managed to halt a robbery.

Of course Mason Riddle did not fit with this group. He was greedy and brutal; seeing an opportunity for illegal gain, he had betrayed his employer without a second thought. Oddly, he was the only one who had actually profited from the robbery along the Fairmont. Until the time of his death. If there was a lesson to be drawn there, it was beyond Laredo.

Now with the sun beginning to lower its head, the day at this altitude became pleasant; not cool, but comfortably warm. There were mountain blue jays chattering in the trees, hopping from branch to branch. Once Laredo saw a badger eye him ferociously and waddle away into the depths of the forest.

Half a mile on he found the man with the blue silk bandanna loose around his throat crouched beside his horse, watching the western approach to the cut-off. Laredo eased his Winchester from its saddle scabbard, slowed his horses and shouted out:

'Just what in hell do you think you're up to, Wilbur!'

Wilbur Harrison rose from his crouch like a man startled from a dream. The blond-haired, spindly youth seemed to consider going for his holstered gun, discarded the thought immediately and said:

'Oh, hello, Laredo. Surprised to see you up here.'

'Not as surprised as I am to see you,' Laredo said roughly. He remained in the saddle, his rifle held loosely across its bow, muzzle aimed in Wilbur Harrison's direction.

Harrison noted the way Laredo was watching

145

him, measured the look in his eyes and the position of the Winchester.

'Laredo, you don't need to have a weapon trained on me,' the young man said innocently, raising both hands for a moment as if the thought was laughable.

'Don't I? What are you doing up here, Wilbur – with that silk scarf around your neck?'

'I. . . .' Wilbur came forward a few steps, looking up pleadingly at Laredo. 'Damnit, Laredo, Calvin Poole fired me! I had just gotten Fortunata's father on my side when it happened. Now what am I supposed to do? I have to marry that woman, Laredo. She's all my hopes wrapped up in one. You see how a man could be driven to it. It's only that I have no other choice. I have an obligation to the girl now.'

Laredo said, 'I don't buy that. But you listen to me – I have an obligation, too. I work for the bank examiner's office, and my job includes protecting what property of theirs I can and tracking down anyone who robs them. You know that.'

'I haven't done anything!' Harrison said, although his plans to do something were all too obvious.

'No, and it's time you did.'

Mystified, Wilbur stared up at Laredo who said, 'You might have gotten away with this, Wilbur, *might* have. If some old hardcase like Andy Patterson is riding shotgun, you wouldn't. You'd hesitate to shoot, Patterson wouldn't. That would be a fine gift to Fortunata, wouldn't it? You shot down along the cut-off, and for what? For trying to hold up a stagecoach from the company you had been working for. That would make her very proud, wouldn't it?'

'You don't understand, Laredo,' Wilbur said in a frustrated croak. 'Calvin Poole—'

'Is an insensitive bastard,' Laredo finished for him. 'Well, so what! That doesn't give you the right to steal from other people. The gold doesn't belong to Poole, you know. It belongs to the banks, and I work for them to make sure things like this don't happen. Besides, Wilbur, you've been around long enough to know – who has ever gotten away with these stick-ups?'

'There's Mason Riddle!' Wilbur blurted out.

'Would you like me to show you where I left his body – in a lonely place where the desert rats are gnawing on his flesh. Besides, Riddle was a thug and a stone-killer. Is that how you want to end up?'

In the distance now Laredo heard the crack of a bullwhip, the squealing of an ungreased wheel hub. The eastbound stage was pulling the long western grade. Wilbur fixed pleading eyes on Laredo.

'What can I do, Laredo?'

'What you set out to do in the first place! Why not flag down the coach, or catch up with it in Flyburg and make your way east, or maybe south to Tucson, to look for work. That was your plan the first time I met you, if I remember.'

'Fortunata. . . .'

'Your marriage might have to be postponed, but at least you'll live long enough to be wed. If she loves you she will wait for you,' Laredo said. 'Whatever you had in mind, it's done now. If the shotgun on the stage doesn't bring you down, I'll do my duty, Wilbur. That's the way things are: a man does his duty.'

Wilbur now glanced westward. The stage could just be seen cresting the ridgeline. 'Think they'll take me aboard?'

'I'll help you with negotiations. Even if you don't have the money, they know you're a former employee. They'll extend that courtesy, I'm sure. Tether your pony on behind the stage and go – just get far away from this country for a while. You can write Fortunata when you have the time, or if you like, I'll swing by and tell her what you had to do.'

'Would you, Laredo?' the young man asked miserably.

'I said I would,' Laredo answered as the stage rounded the last bend, approaching them. 'Now, get that bandanna off your neck and let's halt the coach!'

Laredo stopped at Marshal Donovan's office only in order to report the death of Mason Riddle. Donovan was laconic as usual.

'Well, that's one we don't have to worry about anymore. Have you talked to Calvin Poole?'

'No, and I don't intend to,' Laredo said in measured tones.

'All right. I'll tell him in the morning. I guess that ride to Tres Palmas paid off in the end.'

'I guess it did,' Laredo agreed.

Earlier he had gone to Howard Tibbits's home, the banks being already closed by the time Laredo made it to Mesa. The little man, relaxing after his evening meal, was nevertheless excited enough by Laredo's news to hastily don his coat and travel with Laredo to the First Bank of Mesa, Tibbits's own establishment.

'It's not all here,' Tibbits said after he had totaled up the gold-dust.

'No, it seems that Riddle found someone along his way to exchange a few ounces of dust for cash money – at least he was spending a lot of it in Tres Palmas.'

'Well,' the little banker said, using his thumb to push his spectacles farther up his nose, 'it's certainly more than we expected ever to have returned. I was marking it up in my mind as a dead loss.'

'It nearly was,' Laredo said, sitting on the corner of the counter where the banker had lined up the gold-dust-bearing vials. 'That's a part of what I want to talk to you about.'

'Oh?' Tibbits seemed suddenly wary.

Loredo told him: I didn't recover the gold by myself. I was assisted by Ben Trevor.'

'Trevor?' Tibbits's eyes narrowed behind the lenses of his bifocals. 'No relationship to that highwayman, Hal Trevor?'

'His brother,' Laredo told the banker. 'Ben wanted to try to make amends for his brother's crimes. He volunteered to ride with me in pursuit of Mason Riddle and got himself badly shot up for his trouble.

'Mr Tibbits, I want that man rewarded for what he did.'

'I see. . . .' Tibbits was examining the gold-dust, one jar at a time. 'If you think it's warranted—'

'I do. I can't accept any reward for the recovery of stolen gold, of course, being an agent of the Bank Examiner's office, but Trevor was doing far more than was required of him – in fact the man may not survive his gunshot. I think he deserves something for his efforts.'

'I'll have to talk to the other bankers, of course,' Tibbits said, then he shrugged his round shoulders, 'but otherwise – if things are as you say – we would have recovered nothing. Would five per cent be acceptable, Laredo?'

'I would say that ten per cent would be more acceptable,' Laredo said without smiling. 'You could open an account to draw on with your bank. One other contingency should be provided for – if Ben Trevor does succumb to his wounds, the money should be held for Margarita Trevor.'

'His wife?'

Laredo hesitated only fractionally. 'Yes,' he replied. Telling the banker that the woman was actually the widow of Hal Trevor, the Chicolote Highwayman, could cause problems.

'I'll see that things are drawn up that way,' Tibbits said as Laredo put on his hat and prepared to leave. 'Will you be here in the morning to confirm matters?'

'I sincerely hope not,' Laredo said wearily.

He had only one other stop to make before at last, blessedly, throwing himself on to a bed at the hotel and sleeping long and hard. He rode to the house of Fortunata's family and rapped on the door.

An older man with white hair and a dropping mustache – Fortunata's father, Laredo guessed –

151

opened the door. He was dressed in dark trousers and shirtsleeves. His appraisement of the trail-dusty Laredo was stern.

'I have a message for Fortunata from Wilbur Harrison.'

'What sort of message?'

'I'd like to tell her first, then you can ask her about it,' Laredo said. He was admitted and shown into a large room with a fireplace, unused in this weather, and after a minute a very pretty woman in white was shown in. Dark-haired, dark-eyed, she was younger than Laredo had expected. Harrison had told him she was eighteen, but she looked as if she were fifteen. Small, uncertain, she walked to where Laredo stood before the cold fireplace.

'Father says you have word for me – about Wilbur.' Her eyes showed fear and she clenched her hands together tightly, looking up expectantly at Laredo.

'He's all right,' Laredo said first, to set her mind at ease. 'He has decided to travel south to Tucson probably, where it's easier to find employment.'

'I'm so glad!' Fortunata burst out, surprising Laredo. 'I was so frightened that he would be murdered if he continued driving for that stagecoach line. That was what he wanted to do in the first place, you know – travel to a larger town to find work. It is better that he establish himself in some other business, don't you think?'

'For Wilbur? Yes, I do,' Laredo answered honestly. The job with Poole would have eventually worn the narrow young man down. It wasn't something he was naturally cut out for, just the first opportunity that had offered itself when he needed work.

'And I need a little more time,' Fortunata confided. 'A wedding is an important ceremony in my family, you see. We cannot just run off to a judge. It would kill my mother and anger my father. It is better that we wait. I was too impetuous – both of us were – when we entered so hastily into our agreement.'

'But you love him still?' Laredo asked. 'You plan on waiting for him?'

'Oh, yes!' Fortunata said as if offended by the question. 'He is my man. I will wait for him.'

That settled, Laredo said goodnight and made his way back to the hotel. He hired a boy to take his buckskin and Riddle's white horse to the stable. What happened now to Riddle's horse was none of his affair – Marshal Donovan would have to make that decision.

Laredo made his way up the stairs to the room he had occupied before. His legs felt rubbery under him; a few bumps and bruises he did not remember suffering began to ache as the tension of the day drained from his body. He only managed to take his boots off before the bed summoned him so seductively that it could not be ignored.

# ELEVEN

By the time the sun rose above the eastern horizon, throwing a brief flourish of orange and gold across the sands and the pearly clouds which had returned to the desert, Laredo had already been on the trail for an hour. He had risen wearily and saddled the buckskin while the stars still winked in the deep-blue sky.

Now the land was growing hot again. With various almost imperceptible indications, the horse declared itself to be tired of the long trail, tired of making its way through the deep sand, tired of the constant heat.

When Tres Palmas appeared on the horizon, the squat, shabby collection of adobe buildings was a welcome sight. Laredo knew his way around the tiny village now, and he went first to the small farm where he had sheltered his horse before. The farmer, a wide-grinning man in a huge straw hat, welcomed Laredo and took the buckskin to shelter and water. Laredo made his way across town, keeping to the shade cast by the buildings as much as possible.

Margarita was not inside her house, but the door stood open, so Laredo knocked and entered, calling out to her. He found her behind the house standing near a freshly turned mound of earth marked with a small wooden cross. He approached her, hat in hand. Margarita wore black. Her rounded belly was very evident beneath the fabric. On the lobes of her ears diamonds sparkled in the sunlight. She turned toward him as he approached, her eyes swollen and red.

'Ben?' he asked.

'He only made it back to me. Maria Corona could do nothing for him; he had lost too much blood.'

Ben had realized that he could not hope to survive his wound, Laredo knew. 'He only wanted to see you once more,' he told Margarita.

'I know this.'

A faint, dry wind rose and gusted briefly, shifting an errant strand of dark hair across her forehead.

'I have news for you, Margarita,' Laredo told her. 'Ben only did what he did for your sake and that of the baby. His effort has been rewarded. The bank in Mesa has an account drawn up for you. Any time you are able to get there, they will give you whatever money you need for expenses.'

'That is a relief to know,' Margarita said in an even voice. Her eyes remained fixed on Ben Trevor's grave. 'But was it worth it, Laredo? Was any of this worth it?'

No. It wasn't worth it. Not Hal Trevor's unbridled need for revenge against Calvin Poole – the insult could simply have been ignored, and he could have moved on with his life. Not Ben Trevor's determination to help Margarita and her unborn child through robbery. There were other ways to make money, those that did not snatch your life away from you.

'It wasn't worth it,' Laredo said at last, but Margarita seemed not to have heard his words. He turned then and started back toward the little farm. If the buckskin was not rested fully yet, that was just too bad.

Laredo had a little red-headed wife waiting for him in Crater, and he meant to make his way home to her sooner rather than later.

He had had enough of the desert, and more than enough of the Chicolote Highwaymen.